THE AMISH HOUSEKEEPER

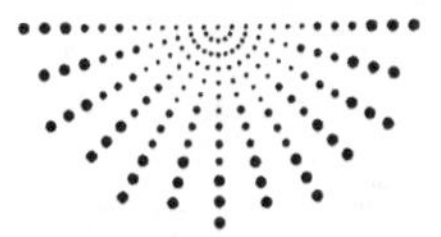

SARAH MILLER

IRENE GLICK

SWEETBOOKHUB.COM

CHAPTER ONE

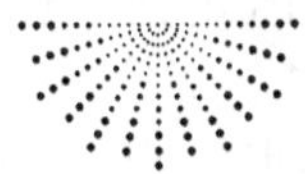

FAITH'S CREEK, PENNSYLVANIA.

"Another bag? How many have we gone through today?" Trina Petersheim asked, as her *mamm*, Rebecca, hauled another load of mending onto the front porch.

It was a hot day in Faith's Creek, a day for lemonade and shade, rather than unstitching and mending. But Trina and her *mamm* had no choice. They were poor, and mending other people's shirts and dresses was the only income they had. Trina's *daed* had died in a buggy accident three years previously, and if it had not been for the kindness of neighbors – whose clothes did not always really need mending – the family would be destitute.

"That's the third today. Harold Holkheim keeps tearing his shirts. Look at this one," Rebecca exclaimed, tutting as she held up a shirt with a tear right along the hem.

Trina shook her head and sighed. They would make only a few dollars from the bag of mending, barely enough to keep food on the table. They lived hand to mouth, relying on their neighbors for a box of vegetables left on the porch or the offer of a buggy ride to the market, where they would sell knitted items for a pittance. It was a hard life, and Trina wished she could do more to help.

She was twenty years old, and her life had turned out very differently from how she had imagined. When her *daed* was alive, the family was prosperous – though never wealthy. He worked repairing buggies and was skilled in carpentry and mechanics. There was nothing he did not know about the undercarriage of a buggy, and people would come from far and wide to seek his skills at repair. After his accident, there was an outpouring of sympathy in Faith's Creek, and much was done by way of charity. But charity can only last so long – life cannot be lived on charity alone.

Trina had imagined marriage, a family, a settled life – this was far from what she had now, and far from what she imagined. Life was hard. She was skilled with a needle and thread, but there were only so many shirts a person could mend in a day. They had tried everything to make money – selling baked goods, growing vegetables, minding other people's *kinner* – but nothing had worked. It seemed this was Trina's destiny, a sad life lived in the sad memory of her *daed's* death. Her *mamm* tried to put on a brave face but she was a broken woman. Trina would often find her crying or simply sitting staring into the distance, lost in her memories.

"I think he does it deliberately. He knows we'd never accept his money for nothing. He tears holes in his shirts and pretends they need mending. He's always been soft on you," Trina replied.

Rebecca blushed. "It's *gut* of him, I'm sure. But a few ripped shirts won't make any difference. I'll need to buy Noah a new pair of shoes this week. Every time I look at him, he grows again," Rebecca replied.

Noah was Trina's younger brother. At fourteen years old, he was still too young to work and attended the schoolhouse on weekdays. He was a boisterous boy, and the death of his *daed* had hit him hard. He could be badly behaved and was always getting into mischief – the latest being the theft of apples from the orchard belonging to their neighbor, Doris Schellter. She had forgiven Noah, but the incident had left a sour taste in her mouth, and Trina was worried as to the direction her brother was taking. He was at an impressionable age, and it would be all too easy for him to take the wrong path for his future.

"We'd better get through this bag before he gets home, then. We'll have no peace when he does," Trina said, threading a needle and taking up one of Harold Holkheim's shirts.

They worked silently for the next hour, deftly mending the shirts and breeches of their friends and neighbors. The items were neatly folded and labeled for return. Trina and her *mamm* prided themselves on their perfect stitching, and by the time Noah returned from the schoolhouse, their day's work was almost done.

"What did you learn at school today, Noah?" Rebecca asked as the boy ran up onto the porch.

"Oh... something about numbers, I don't know. I want some lemonade," he said, spying the jug Trina had made up earlier.

"Now, Noah, you know better than to speak like that," Trina said, giving her brother a warning glance.

He was regularly forgetting his manners, and Trina was determined to instill some discipline into him. She could only imagine what their *daed* would say if he had been there.

"Can I have some lemonade, please?" Noah said.

Rebecca winked at Trina and poured him a glass. "You've got to work hard at school, Noah. It's no good coming back each day and forgetting everything. You need education to get a job. No one's going to employ a young man who doesn't apply himself," she said, glancing at Trina, this time, with a worried expression on her face.

It was a worry Trina shared. They could not support themselves with bags of mending forever. When Noah finished school, he needed a job. Trina and Rebecca did their best but they could not go on providing for him — he was their hope, too.

"I'll be a laborer on one of the farms. I don't care. I hate school," Noah retorted, taking the glass from their *mamm*, who shook her head sadly.

"Your *daed* wouldn't want you to say that, Noah. He worked hard at school. He learned mechanics and book-keeping. He was interested in the world around him..." she began, but Noah interrupted her.

"Well, he's not here, is he?" he said, and then he stormed off into the house, leaving Trina and her *mamm* on the porch.

There were tears in Rebecca's eyes. Trina reached out and took her by the hand.

"Don't get upset, *Mamm*. You know what he's like. He'll calm down. He's at that age," Trina said.

Rebecca nodded. "I'm so lucky to have you, Trina. I don't know what I'd do without you. I couldn't cope with him," she said, sighing as she began to fold the last of the shirts.

At that moment, the click of the garden gate caused them both to look up. Sarah Beiler, the *fraa* of Bishop Beiler, was coming up the garden path. She was carrying a casserole dish, and she smiled at Trina as she went to meet her.

"This is an unexpected pleasure," Trina said, as Sarah handed her the casserole.

"I was making one for Amos, and I thought I might as well do two as the oven was on. It's just chicken and vegetables, but I know Noah could eat a whole one and still have room for more. I thought it might help," she said.

Trina nodded.

Ever since the death of her *daed*, Bishop Beiler and Sarah had been unfailingly kind. Trina and her *mamm* did all their mending, and Sarah often appeared with a casserole or a batch of cookies. She knew the troubles they were having with Noah and had been a great support to them all.

"That's very kind of you, Sarah," Rebecca said, coming to greet her.

"I see you've been busy this afternoon," Sarah said, glancing at the piles of mending.

"Three bags of shirts and breeches. I don't know what people in Faith's Creek do all day, but they certainly get a lot of holes in their clothes!" Rebecca chuckled.

Sarah laughed, and they invited her to join them on the porch for a glass of lemonade. Trina brought out the remnants of a seed cake and they made a happy party, catching up with the goings on around the community.

"There was something else I wanted to talk to you about," Sarah said after they had finished their refreshments.

"It's not Noah, is it? He's not been misbehaving again, has he?" The worry on Rebecca's face was clear.

Sarah shook her head. "*Nee*, nothing like that. It's a proposition for Trina," she replied.

Trina looked up at her in surprise. "Something for the church?" she asked.

Her faith meant everything to her. If it had not been for the church, she would never have coped with the loss of her *daed*. Prayer was a refuge for her, and she had learned to trust in *Gott* and offer up her troubles to *Gott* whenever she was in need.

"*Nee.* It's a job, actually. There's an *Englischer* by the name of Ernest Lindorp. He's taken the house on Forest Hill. He was a professor of some kind, and he's come to Faith's Creek in retirement. He and Amos had a long discussion the other day, and he mentioned he was looking for a housekeeper. I thought of you, Trina," she said.

Trina looked at her in surprise. She and her *mamm* had tried so many ways to make ends meet, but the thought of taking a job like this had never occurred to her. Faith's Creek was the sort of place where people made money themselves, rather than working for others. There were laborers on the farms, but they were men, and Trina had never heard of anyone in the district having a housekeeper.

"Me? Do you think I could?" she replied.

Sarah Beiler nodded. "I think you'd be perfect, and I told the professor as much," she replied.

Trina smiled, this could make all the difference to them. "Then I'll give it some thought," she said, even as her mind was already made up.

CHAPTER TWO

"I'm just not sure about it, Trina. An *Englischer*? A professor? We don't know anything about him," Rebecca said.

Sarah Beiler had left, having given further details of the professor's situation. It would not be a live-in job – the house on Forest Hill was only a mile or so away – and Trina would be expected to cook, clean, mend, and undertake whatever domestic tasks were required. There was no doubt in Trina's mind that she could do it and do it well.

She would earn enough to support the whole family, enough so that her *mamm* would no longer need to take in mending. It would be enough to provide Noah with the things he needed for school and to make a good start in life. Maybe even enough to save a little.

"Just because he's an *Englischer* doesn't mean there's something to fear from him," Trina replied.

She had never understood the fear amongst some of the community of outsiders. Bishop Beiler clearly thought him a decent sort, and so did Sarah. That was enough for Trina, and she had already decided to accept the job.

"Well... I don't know," Rebecca replied, but Trina was adamant this was what she wanted.

Besides, there was little choice but to accept, and the next day, Trina went to call on Sarah Beiler, and arrangements were made for the two of them to visit the professor at his house on Forest Hill.

Trina was nervous. She wanted to make a good impression and dressed in her Sunday best – her newest blue dress, a white apron, and a freshly pressed *kapp*. Sarah called for her later that afternoon and the two of them set off for the short walk to Forest Hill.

The house was a remnant from the earliest days of Faith's Creek, wood slat and surrounded by tall trees and a mature garden. A veranda ran around three sides, with steps leading up to a large front door. It was a house far too big for one person, and Trina was not surprised the professor needed a housekeeper.

"Why did he move here?" Trina asked as the two of them walked up the path towards the house.

"He wanted peace and quiet for his work. He taught at Harvard, I believe. He's a historian of the early settlers, American history, that sort of thing. I suppose our way of life reminded him of the history he's studied. I don't know much more about him, though, but he seems a nice man. I think you'll get along. Amos is here, too," Sarah replied.

They made their way up the steps, and Sarah knocked at the door. Trina smoothed down her dress, trying not to appear nervous as footsteps could be heard from inside. An elderly-looking man opened the door. He looked like a professor, his half-moon spectacles perched on his nose. He had a white beard and twinkling blue eyes and was dressed formally in a jacket, shirt, tie, cords, and a pair of brown shoes.

"Ah, Mrs. Beiler, how good to see you, and this must be Miss Petersheim," he said, smiling at Trina, who nodded.

"Just Trina, please, Professor Lindorp," she said, as he ushered them inside.

"I'm sure we'll get used to one another, and…" he began, but his words were interrupted by violent coughing, and he pulled a spotted handkerchief from his pocket and held it to his mouth.

"Are you all right?" Sarah asked, patting him on the back.

"Oh… yes, quite all right. Just a frog in my throat. We've been talking about the first settlers in Faith's Creek. I've got quite excited hearing all about the history of this place," the professor said, just as Bishop Beiler emerged from a door into the hallway.

Trina had always liked Bishop Amos Beiler. He had been the first to visit them on the day her *daed* had died, and he had been a steadying influence on Noah, too.

"It's good to see you, Trina. I know you'll be a great help to the professor," Amos said.

Trina felt heat hit her cheeks at such a compliment. "That's if I've got the job," she said, glancing at the professor.

"You've come highly recommended. I don't take much looking after. A light lunch, something for dinner, the house dusted, the bed made, a little mending, the washing done. Like all academics, I can be a little absent-minded – just keep me on the straight and narrow," he replied with a smile.

Trina had not encountered many *Englischers* before. The inhabitants of Faith's Creek had always been Amish. The community was settled by Trina's ancestors, and it had a long history associated with the Amish faith. To meet an outsider who wanted to become part of that was strange, even though Trina could understand the professor's reasons for doing so.

"I'll happily do all those things. You'll have to tell me the sort of things you like to eat. Not everyone likes buttered noodles and shoofly pie," Trina said.

Her nerves were gone. She had warmed to the professor and the thought of working for him was a prospect she looked forward to.

"I like plain food. Nothing fancy. You'll find I'm happiest with a lamb cutlet and a few potatoes and vegetables. There's no shortage of farms around here. We'll manage just fine. I'm partial to an apple fritter, though," he said.

"Who isn't?" Trina smiled. "I can make apple fritters."

They were Noah's favorites and her brother always insisted on them for breakfast on a Saturday morning.

"Then that's settled," the professor replied.

He gave her a brief tour of the house. It was filled with books – shelves, boxes, piles. They were everywhere. It would all need sorting out, and Trina resolved to set about doing so the following day. Everywhere was dusty, too, and she wondered if the professor's cough was down to the layers of dust on every surface, dust which blew up in great clouds at the slightest movement.

"I can start first thing tomorrow," she said, as the professor showed her out.

"That would be fine. We can talk about your hours and pay then," he said, and to her surprise, he slipped a ten-dollar bill into her hand.

"But I've not done anything yet," she protested.

Professor Lindorp smiled at her. "I'm just pleased to have found someone," he said, even as he began to cough again.

Trina left in high spirits with Sarah Beiler. Bishop Beiler had remained – a high brow conversation now occurring over the religious practices of the early settlers in Faith's Creek.

"I think it's going to work out well for everyone," Sarah said, as she and Trina made their way back towards Trina's house.

"I think so, too. That house needs a good clean first. No wonder he coughs so much with all that dust in the air," Trina replied, and Sarah nodded.

They parted ways close to Trina's house, and Trina hurried home, excited to tell her *mamm* about the professor and the opportunities afforded her. But as she approached the house, Trina saw a familiar figure on the porch, sitting with her *mamm* and shaking her head, the two of them deep in conversation. It was her aunt, Leah Speicher, and as Trina approached, she looked up and tutted.

"What's all this about you working for an *Englischer?*" she demanded.

Trina sighed, knowing what came next would not be easy.

CHAPTER THREE

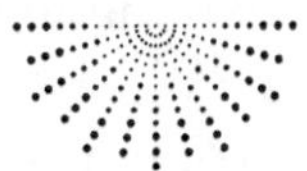

Trina's aunt was not happy. She objected to Trina working for an *Englischer* and was not afraid to speak her mind.

"It's a betrayal of our values, Trina. Outsiders mean trouble. I don't trust someone like that, and neither should you. If I'd known about it before, I'd have put a stop to it right away," she said, glancing at Rebecca, who seemed powerless in the face of her sister's overbearing nature.

"But... Leah... we need the money. This man... this professor, he's going to pay Trina well. She wants to do it," Rebecca said.

Trina was grateful to her *mamm* for siding with her – albeit reluctantly.

"We've always managed, haven't we? You've got two bags of mending there. Whilst she's been off at Forest Hill, there's no money been made here," Leah retorted.

Leah was a formidable woman. Large in stature as well as in opinion. She was three years older than Rebecca and married to a man named John. They had no *kinner*, and Trina's aunt had made it her business to interfere in the raising of Trina and Noah. When Noah had stolen the apples, it was his Aunt Leah who had punished him, and his Uncle John who had seen to it he realized the consequences of stealing.

"He gave me ten dollars just for taking the time to visit today," Trina said, holding out the ten-dollar bill for her aunt and *mamm* to see.

Her Aunt Leah sniffed.

"*Englischer* money," said replied.

Trina rolled her eyes. "What does it matter? He's a nice man, it won't be a difficult job. He just needs someone to take care of him, that's all," she said, and her aunt narrowed her eyes suspiciously.

"I don't think it's appropriate, Rebecca. A young woman like Trina working alone in the house of an older man. You don't know what his motives are," she said, even as Trina protested.

"I think his motives are a desire for a clean house and someone to cook his meals for him. He's an academic. He reads books all day. Besides, it was Bishop Beiler and Sarah who suggested it. Don't you think they might know what's best for me, too?" Trina had her hand on her hips as she asked the question.

The mention of Bishop Beiler caused her aunt to falter. She could hardly accuse the leader of the community of a lack of morals. But she remained adamant that Trina working for an *Englischer* was wrong.

"I just don't like it, Trina. It's not our way," she said, folding her arms.

Trina knew there would be no changing her aunt's mind. Leah was stubborn, and even when she knew she was wrong, she would not admit it.

"I'm going to work for him. I'm going to give it a chance. We won't need to take in mending now. *Mamm* can look after Noah and I'll support us with my wage," Trina said, knowing her plan made sense.

"A girl of your age – a woman – should be looking for a husband," Leah said,

Biting back a sigh, Trina realized the truth behind her aunt's objections.

With her aunt, the subject always turned to marriage. With the death of her *daed* and the uncertainty of their situation, Trina had found little time to think of marriage or courtship. There were men in Faith's Creek she found attractive, and men who found her attractive, too. But she had found little time to pursue such things and had pushed the matter aside, along with the interested men, preferring to concentrate on more practical matters. But her aunt was persistent, and whenever she visited – which was often, for she only lived a short distance away – mention would be made of Trina's future.

"We've been through this, Aunt Leah," Trina replied, but her aunt tutted.

"But this time, I have a proposition to make. John's just taken on a new laborer for the small holding. He's a nice young man by the name of Elmer Renno. He's unattached, he's attractive – he'd be perfect for you," Leah said.

Trina had to smile at the thought of her aunt's simplistic criterion for marriage. Unattached and attractive did not mean the immediacy of falling in love, even as her aunt seemed to believe the matter was simple. Trina remembered Elmer Renno from school. He was a pleasant enough sort, though she could not remember having anything more than a casual acquaintance with him. He had worked as a laborer on any number of farms, but apart from that, she really knew nothing more about him.

"I don't know... does he even want to meet someone?" Trina asked.

It was one thing to suggest the possibility of a match, but quite another to do so if neither of the parties was interested. They had been here before. Her aunt would suggest a possibility, and Trina would reject it. The men her aunt chose were the dependable sort, reliable, and... well, dull.

There had been Simon Schleig, who worked in the bookstore and had spent the entire duration of their somewhat artificial meeting explaining the cataloging system he had devised in place of a previous one, which confused archaeology with anthropology. Then there had been David Holstein, a pleasant man, who collected butterflies. They had found little in common save a liking for pear drops, and the encounter had ended with David promising to take Trina butterfly catching – an event which was still to occur.

"He might not realize he wants to meet someone," Leah replied.

Trina smiled. "That's not quite the same thing," she said, but her aunt's mind was already made up.

"We'll arrange something – get the two of you together. It'll be *gut* for you, Trina," she said.

Trina sighed.

There was no point in arguing, but she was determined to hold her own when it came to the job with the professor.

"All right. I'll meet him. But I'm going to work for Professor Lindorp, and that's final. We need the money and I like him. He's already treated me well. I won't be told I can't," she said, glancing at her *mamm* with a defiant expression.

"It'll come to no good. Mark my words," Leah replied, but she made no further attempt to dissuade Trina from what she was determined to do, and it seemed the matter was settled.

It was not that Trina was averse to the idea of romance. She wanted to get married. She wanted a family. She wanted to be happy. But such artificial encounters seemed far from the ideal, and she was already convinced that meeting Elmer Renno would be just the same as meeting all the others.

"*Just humor her,*" she told herself, grateful at least that her aunt's opposition to her work for the professor had been placated.

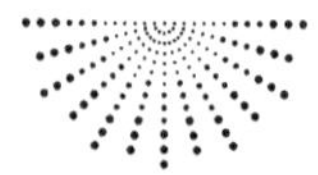

CHAPTER FOUR

The next morning, Trina rose bright and early for her first day of work for the professor. She had laid out a clean dress and *kapp* the night before and intended to be at the house on Forest Hill in time to make the professor's breakfast. He had given her a key, telling her to come and go as she pleased. Trina wanted to prove herself to him, and she had spent the previous evening reading through her *mamm's* cookbooks and devising menus to serve the professor for lunch and dinner.

"I think I'll make pancakes for his breakfast... oh, I hope he's been to the store. What if there's nothing there?" Trina said, as her *mamm* entered the parlor.

"Take the ingredients from here. We won't miss a few eggs and some flour – not when we have a wage soon to come," she said.

Trina did as she suggested, feeling a little better that she would be organized.

She set off for Forest Hill with a bag containing eggs, flour, and a bottle of milk. It was still early, and she met no one on the way, approaching the house and seeing the shutters were still closed. She felt nervous at the thought of her first day at work. Life would be very different from now on, but Trina was looking forward to doing all she could to make the professor comfortable and feel at home. Letting herself in through the side door, she made her way to the kitchen, listening for any sounds from above.

"Let's see, now. It's all quite different, isn't it?" she said to herself, looking around the kitchen, which had been fitted with all manner of modern appliances.

There was a fridge, a freezer, a microwave, a gas oven, and all sorts of other appliances with which Trina was unfamiliar. She set down her bag and rolled up her sleeves before straightening her apron and setting to work.

The pancake batter was soon mixed, but she had trouble lighting the stove and burned the first of the pancakes to a cinder.

"I thought I could smell burning," a voice in the doorway said.

Trina turned in horror to find the professor standing there. "Oh... I'm sorry. I thought I'd surprise you. I'm making pancakes... though not very well," she said.

The professor smiled. "Don't worry. I usually just have oatmeal for breakfast. I swear by it," he said.

Trina breathed a sigh of relief.

"It's just, I'm not used to all these modern appliances. We don't use anything electrical," she said, glancing warily at the microwave.

"It's all right. You don't have to use them. I bought them because I thought I'd be taking care of myself. I'm not used to cooking. Back at Harvard, I had a housekeeper, too, you see," he said.

Trina nodded. "I'll learn, I'm sure. But... perhaps I'll stick to what I know," she said.

She was relieved at the professor's words. She knew what her aunt would say about a microwave, and now she set about preparing a tray with a bowl of oatmeal and a strong pot of coffee, just as the professor directed. She could hear him coughing in the dining room, and the sound reminded her to set about dusting the whole house from top to bottom.

"It must be catching," she said to herself, feeling her nose tickled from the dust which danced in the steams of sunlight coming through the hallway windows as she took the professor his breakfast

He was sitting at the far end of the table, by the window, in the dining room. He was reading a book, and he looked up at her and smiled as she entered the room.

"We can try pancakes another day. A bowl of oatmeal will do just fine, thank you. I'll be in my study for most of the morning, but don't hesitate to disturb me if you need anything," he said.

Trina set the tray down in front of him and nodded.

"What made you come to Faith's Creek, Professor?" she asked, as she poured out a cup of coffee for him.

"Oh, I've long been interested in these communities. They're living history. The way of life, the traditions, the customs. I've spent so long writing about the early settlers, but to experience something of their way of life for myself... was too good an opportunity to miss. Retirement beckoned, and I saw this house for sale the last time I passed through – Bishop Beiler and I are old friends," he said, lifting his cup.

He took a sip and then began to cough.

Trina looked at him anxiously. "Are you all right?" she asked.

He nodded, waving his hand until he could speak. "It's just a tickle in my throat. It's nothing to worry about."

Trina wondered if those words were meant for his benefit or hers. It was a nasty cough and she resolved to clean the whole house from top to bottom immediately.

"I'm going to dust. I won't move anything, but I'm going to clean the whole house," she said, with a resolute determination in her voice.

The professor nodded. "I think we're going to get along just fine, Trina," he replied.

At that moment, a shrill noise filled the air, and Trina jumped out of her skin, even as Professor Lindorp laughed.

"It's just the telephone ringing. I don't answer it, though. It's usually someone trying to sell me something. I prefer writing letters. If someone really wants to speak to me, they'll do the same. I'm sorry, I forgot you'd not be used to the sound," he said.

Trina laughed, even as her heart was beating fast – microwaves, telephones, a radio – she was going to have to get used to them all.

The rest of the morning was spent dusting. Trina was systematic and tackled one room at a time. The house was sprawling and spread over three floors. A dining room, best parlor, kitchen, study, and pantry made up the first floor, whilst on the second, Professor Lindorp had a den and a library room, along with three bedrooms and a bathroom. The third floor was given over to four more bedrooms, and two bathrooms, whilst a basement contained three storerooms, all of which smelled of damp and were filled with junk leftover from the previous occupants. But it was the books that took the longest to dust.

"Achoo!" Trina exclaimed, sneezing violently in a cloud of dust.

She was balancing on a footstool to reach the very highest of the shelves in the library. She had opened all the windows, and the breeze blowing in from outside swirled up the dust in a great cloud, so that again she sneezed, coughing and spluttering as she climbed down from the step ladder.

"This is going to take longer than a day," she told herself, resigned to tackling a room at a time.

It was nearly lunch time and she hurried to the kitchen, intent on making the professor something he would actually enjoy. She eyed the microwave warily – all those buttons, and the electricity. It made her uncomfortable and she turned her back on it, concentrating instead on the stove, which she lit, before examining the cupboards to see what she might make. There was shopping to be done, and it was clear the professor gave little thought to his meals or what he ate. But there were some dried noodles, and the flour, eggs, and butter left over from the earlier attempt at pancakes – all of which could be put to good use. In the pantry, Trina found a store of apples and a rack of spices.

"Buttered noodles and apple fritters," she said out loud, pleased to have found something she could make with little difficulty.

Half an hour later, Trina proudly presented the professor with his lunch. He had spent the morning reading, and he smiled at Trina as he sat down at the dining room table and examined the dishes before him.

"It looks delicious. You told me you'd make apple fritters – your brother's favorites?" he said.

Trina nodded. "Noah loves apple fritters – and buttered noodles, and just about anything else that's put in front of him. He's a growing boy, but I don't know where he puts it," she said, smiling at the thought of Noah's appetite.

The professor helped himself to the dish of buttered noodles, taking a forkful from his plate and pronouncing them to be delicious.

"My son was the same. He just ate and ate and ate. I suppose that's what growing boys do," he said.

Trina was surprised to hear him mention a son. She had not even thought the professor had been married, let alone that he had *kinner*. She had assumed him to be a bachelor – too taken up with his books to think much about anything else.

"Will your son visit you here?" she asked, helping the professor to an apple fritter.

He looked suddenly sad and shook his head.

"He's very busy. He's a lawyer in Philadelphia. He doesn't have much time for visiting," he replied, and before Trina could reply, he had begun to cough, holding up his napkin to his mouth.

"Oh, let me get you some water," she exclaimed, hurrying to fetch a glass and jug from the kitchen.

By the time she returned, the professor had recovered himself, but his face was red, and he thanked her for the water, pushing the half-eaten apple fritter aside.

"I'll finish it later. Why don't you get off home, Trina? You've been a great help to me today. I'm sure we're going to get on just fine. I'll see you tomorrow," he said, taking a sip of water from the glass and giving her a weak smile.

As Trina finished clearing up in the kitchen she wondered about the professor's cough. She had put it down to dust, but it seemed more than that – persistent and unpleasant.

"*I hope it's nothing serious,*" she said to herself, as she made her way home, wondering if the professor's son knew anything about his *daed's* illness...

CHAPTER FIVE

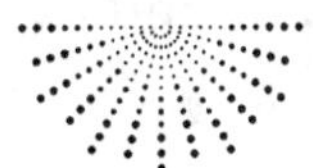

"I'll make a rice salad, everyone likes a rice salad," Rebecca said, as she and Trina prepared for the cookout at Trina's aunt's house.

"Cookout" was another name for a staged introduction. It was always the same. Leah would take it on herself to find Trina a suitable match. She and John would hold a cookout on their smallholding. The neighbors would be invited and there would be an abundance of food – but all of that would be merely stage dressing. The point of the cookout was simple – an introduction between Trina and whichever man her aunt had decided was right for her. Trina knew the drill – it was always the same.

"I don't think it matters what you make. Aunt Leah won't mind if you don't make anything. She just wants to introduce me to Elmer Renno, that's all," Trina replied.

It was a week since her aunt had first mentioned the name of Elmer as a suitor and during that time, she had extolled his virtues at every opportunity. Whilst Trina was not averse to meeting him or reacquainting herself with him, the thought of anything more was far from her mind. Trina was content as she was, and she was very much enjoying her new job as the professor's house-keeper. Today was her day and the professor had handed her an envelope with her wages, along with a bonus to treat herself with.

"I've never been so well looked after," he had told her, having pronounced everything she made to be delicious.

"Don't you want to meet Elmer again?" her *mamm* asked, as she began to make the rice salad.

"I don't know... it all seems so artificial," Trina replied, sighing with resignation as to her fate to come.

She could picture the scene well enough – tables laid out under the trees in her aunt's orchard, her uncle's work-ers, and the neighbors milling about. Elmer would be introduced and the two of them would strike up an awkward conversation that would last until the ordeal was over. Then they would go their separate ways and a few months later, Trina's aunt would suggest a new suitor and the cycle would begin again.

"At least give him a go, Trina. You never know, you might like him. You're such a pretty girl. It's such a shame for you to be on your own," her *mamm* replied.

Trina smiled. "I don't mind. We've had plenty of other things to think about over these past few years. When the right man comes along, I'll know it," she said, confident in *Gott's* plans for her future.

The rice salad joined a myriad of other dishes on the long trestle table in the orchard of Leah and John's smallholding.

It was a hot day, and Trina was glad of the shade from the trees. It was just as she had imagined – tables groaning with food, the neighbors arriving one by one, and her aunt playing hostess.

Noah had been instructed to hand around the drinks and had just poured Trina a glass of lemonade when she spotted Elmer Renno coming through the orchard gate.

He was much as she remembered him, though grown taller since their schooldays. He had a pleasant face and dusty blonde hair. He was dressed in a checked shirt and his face was tanned and attractive. Leah went to greet him, and Trina knew it would only be a matter of moments before the introductions were made.

"He looks like a nice boy, Trina," Rebecca whispered.

Trina smiled. "I'm sure he is," she replied, as now her aunt – leading Elmer by the arm – approached.

Elmer was blushing and Trina knew he, too, knew just what her aunt had planned.

"Trina, this is Elmer. He's just started laboring for your uncle. Elmer, this is my niece, Trina. She's been eager to meet you," Leah said, and with that, she pulled Rebecca away, leaving Trina and Elmer alone under one of the apple trees.

Elmer smiled at her.

"It's *gut* to see you again. I don't think we've spoken since school," he said.

Trina laughed. "Did we really speak much at school? It doesn't matter, though. I'm glad to speak to you now, I guess." She gave him a conspiring smile.

It was one thing to find her aunt's behavior exasperating, but quite another to be rude. Trina was always willing to give these matches the time of day, even if so far they had all turned out to be wanting. She was interested in Elmer and curious to know more about him, for despite them having been acquainted since *kinnerhood*, Trina really knew little about him.

"Your aunt told me you've just started working for the *Englischer* on Forest Hill. What's that like?" he asked.

"Oh, I like it. He's really nice. It's a remarkable house – filled with all kinds of gadgets and gizmos. Not that I've used them, of course," she said.

He laughed. "Shall we get something to eat? I've been working on the smallholding all morning. I'm famished," he said, eyeing the table laden with food.

They helped themselves from the vast array of dishes and returned to the spot under the apple tree. Trina was surprised at how much she was enjoying Elmer's company. He was easy to get along with and asked her questions, rather than talking about himself. It was a refreshing change.

"Do you like working for my uncle?" she asked.

Elmer nodded. "He's a *gut* man, and he lets me go riding if I've finished all my jobs."

Trina's interest was piqued. She loved horses, even if the possibility of owning one was far out of her reach. When her *daed* had been alive, they had owned two horses – Pledge and Bolt – and Trina's *daed* would often accompany her on long rides onto the ridge above Faith's Creek. These were amongst her most precious memories, but the horses had been sold in the aftermath of the accident, and it seemed unlikely Trina would ever ride again.

"You ride?" she asked, and Elmer nodded.

"I love to. I've got my own horse. He's called Starlight. He's fast. Would you like to see him sometime?" he asked.

Trina nodded. "I'd love to. We had our own horses – Pledge and Bolt. My *daed* was a buggy repairer, but he drove them, too. I used to ride with him," she said, suddenly feeling tears rising in her eyes.

"I'm sorry. I know your *daed* died in a buggy accident. It can't be easy talking about it," he said.

Trina shook her head. "It's all right. I don't mind. It's *gut* to talk about him. They were happy times. I'd love to meet Starlight. Where do you ride him?" she asked.

"Up onto the ridge, mostly. You should see him when he gets going. A full gallop. It's quite something," he said, grinning at her.

To Trina's surprise, the two of them passed a very pleasant afternoon together. No one disturbed them as they sat beneath the apple tree, and when Rebecca came to tell her it was time to go home, Trina found herself reluctant to leave.

"It's been really nice meeting you properly," she said, as they rose to their feet.

"It has. I'm glad your aunt arranged this," Elmer replied.

He looked suddenly embarrassed, as though uncertain of what he should say or do next. But it was Trina who took the initiative – much to her own surprise.

"I hope I'll get to meet Starlight soon. You should bring him up here one afternoon. The professor usually lets me leave after lunch. I just leave his dinner under a plate. We could ride out one time – if you don't mind double saddling," she said.

Elmer smiled. "I don't mind at all. I'll bring him. Maybe one day next week?" he said, and now the two of them bid one another goodbye.

"He seemed very nice, Trina," Rebecca said, as they returned home.

Trina smiled. She had surprised herself that afternoon and there was no denying her *mamm* was right.

"He was," she replied, wondering where such thoughts might take her...

CHAPTER SIX

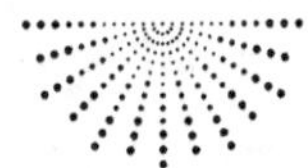

"That's the last of them," Trina said, shaking her duster out of the open window and turning to the professor with a look of satisfaction on her face.

The books were dusted – every last one. She had finished every shelf, carefully replacing them in just the right order. There was not a speck of dust anywhere, and Trina looked around proudly at her accomplishment.

The professor smiled.

"I've found books I'd forgotten I had. When I arrived here, I just had the removal men put them on the shelves. They came off dusty in Massachusetts and went on dusty here in Faith's Creek. You've worked wonders," he said.

Trina laughed. "It's just a bit of polish and elbow grease, Professor. I'd better start lunch," she replied.

Thanks to her *mamm's* cookbooks, Trina had developed a repertoire of recipes to tempt the professor's palate. There was nothing she made he did not pronounce as being delicious, but his favorite remained buttered noodles, followed by apple fritters. It was these dishes she prepared today, serving them to the professor in the dining room a short while later. He had been coughing violently, and she brought him a jug of water and a glass, watching anxiously as he took a drink.

"Thank you, Trina. I'm expecting a visitor this afternoon. You don't have to stay," he said, his face red from coughing.

"It's no trouble. I've got plenty of jobs to do. I can make coffee for you, and I've just put some cinnamon buns in the oven. They'll be delicious, just warm. Is it Bishop Beiler? He's very partial to a cinnamon bun," Trina said, serving Professor Lindorp a portion of buttered noodles.

He shook his head.

"No, it's not Bishop Beiler, though I'm expecting him tomorrow. You can stay if you like. But we don't need any refreshments," he replied.

Trina nodded. She was curious to know who the visitor would be. On the whole, the attitude in Faith's Creek towards the professor was one of suspicion. Like Trina's aunt, most of her neighbors viewed the professor as an outsider, and outsiders were not welcome.

"I'll listen out for the door," Trina replied, and she returned to the kitchen just as the cinnamon buns were ready.

A short while after lunch, Trina heard a knock at the door, and she hurried into the hallway to open it. To her surprise, she found Doctor Yoder, Faith's Creek's resident physician, standing on the porch with his medical bag. He smiled at her and nodded.

"I've come to see Professor Lindorp, Trina. Sarah Beiler told me you were working here. Is it going well?" he asked.

Trina nodded as a seed of worry planted in her stomach.

"Come in, Doctor Yoder. Yes, it's going very well. I really like working for the professor. But is something wrong?" she asked, thinking immediately of the professor's cough.

Doctor Yoder shook his head.

"It's too early to say. Better to be certain. I'd better make my house call, though," he replied, stepping into the hallway.

"He's in the dining room. Would you like some coffee, Doctor Yoder?" Trina asked, feeling anxious at the thought of something being wrong with the professor, just as she had suspected.

"*Nee, denke.* I have a few more calls to make after this, too," he replied.

Trina showed him into the dining room. She lingered outside the door, even as she knew it was wrong to listen at keyholes. But she was worried about the professor and anxious to do whatever she could to help.

"Am I dying, Doctor Yoder?" Trina heard the professor ask, and her heart skipped a beat.

"Not just yet, Professor Lindorp, but you've got a nasty and persistent cough. It's easy for these things to develop into something worse. Were you a smoker in your younger days?" Doctor Yoder replied.

"It was fashionable at one time. But no, I never really smoked, except on occasion. My wife hated the smell," Professor Lindorp replied.

Trina listened as the doctor made some further examinations.

"There're still some tests I want to conduct. I'll need to check a few things and come back in a few days. I'm not certain what's wrong with you, Professor Lindorp. But my advice is to take things easy. Don't exert yourself too much," Doctor Yoder said.

Trina hurried back to the kitchen, not wishing to be caught listening at the door. She heard the professor ushering the doctor out and the opening and closing of the door onto the porch. Tears were welling up in her eyes and she found herself quite overcome by the thought of the professor's illness. She barely knew him, but the thought of his being ill reminded her of her *daed*. How fragile life could be, and she wondered again about his son, and whether he knew anything of his *daed's* illness.

"Could I have some coffee, Trina? Thank you," the professor said, poking his head into the kitchen a moment later.

Trina wiped her sleeves across her eyes.

"Oh… certainly, Professor Lindorp. I'll bring you some cinnamon buns, too. I've just dusted them with sugar," she said, hoping the professor would not notice the tears in her eyes.

A few moments later, Trina had composed herself, and she carried a tray with a pot of coffee and a plate of cinnamon buns into the professor's study. He was sitting in an armchair reading a book and he looked up at her and nodded. There was a strange expression on his face. A look of sad resignation. She poured him out a cup of coffee and set it down on the table next to him.

"I'm not sure what to think," Professor Lindorp said.

Trina felt confused. "What about, Professor?" she asked.

The professor sighed.

"What Doctor Yoder just told me. You've heard me coughing enough to know something's wrong. I ignored it for long enough, but it wasn't getting any better. He's got to run some more tests. I'm not used to being ill. I've got through my whole life without ever having a stay in hospital – except for having my tonsils out. I'm not used to being a patient," he said, and now he began to cough, his whole body shuddering as Trina rushed to fetch some water for him.

"Oh… I'm sorry. You don't have to suffer alone, though, Professor. I'm here to take care of you, and you've got your son, too," Trina said.

But at the mention of his son, Professor Lindorp shook his head and sighed.

"Well… we don't talk very much, that's the thing. He's busy, he's got his own life and I've got mine. It's not worth disturbing him for something as trivial as this…" he began.

Trina disagreed. "Trivial? There's something wrong with you, Professor Lindorp, you've got a terrible cough and until Doctor Yoder finds out what it is, you need looking after. That's not trivial. He'd want to know, sure-ly," she exclaimed, shaking her head in astonishment at the thought of keeping the professor's son in the dark.

But the professor only sighed.

"It's not as simple as that, Trina. The two of us had a… well, a disagreement. We never got on very well. But my wife always played the peacemaker. We're too much alike – stubborn and set in our ways." He shook his head and looked both sad and defeated. It almost broke her heart. "We've drifted apart over the past few years, and me coming to live out here... well, I've not exactly made it easy for him, have I?"

There was a sadness in his voice, a sadness which made Trina feel terribly sorry for him. She could not imagine being at odds with any of her family. She and her aunt had their disagreements, but there was no doubting the love they had for one another. The thought of the professor and his son being estranged filled her with pity, and Trina wondered if there was something she could do to help.

"Perhaps not... but it's never too late to mend a broken relationship," she said.

The professor only shook his head.

"I don't know. Anyway... these cinnamon buns look delicious. Why don't you get yourself off home, Trina? I'll see you tomorrow."

As Trina made her way home that afternoon, she could not help but feel sad at the thought of the professor all alone and his son knowing nothing of the illness that afflicted him.

"I just think he deserves to know," she told her *mamm* later that evening, having explained the situation to her.

"It's their choice, Trina," Rebecca replied, but Trina's mind was already made up – she was going to reunite *daed* and son, eager to prove her worth and do something *gut* in the face of the looming problems ahead.

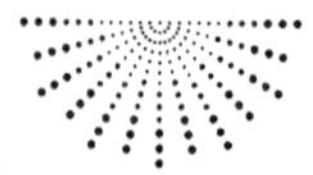

CHAPTER SEVEN

Elmer Reddo was brushing down his horse. Starlight was standing patiently. Elmer took a sugar lump from his pocket and held it out for the horse to snaffle.

"*Gut* boy, you're looking sleek. I can't wait to show you off to Trina," Elmer said, patting the horse's bay neck beneath his black mane.

Starlight was central to Elmer's plan. He had been trying to pluck up the courage to speak to Trina again for the past five days. Meeting her at the cookout had been a revelation. He had not thought of her since their schooldays, and when his new employer, John Speicher, had mentioned his niece, Elmer had shown little enthusiasm at the thought of an introduction.

But the Speichers had been kind to him, and he had wanted to make a *gut* impression and did not wish to appear ungrateful. He had been nervous at first, but Trina had soon set him at ease, and he had found the afternoon spent in her company a delight.

"I just wish I knew what to do next," he said to himself, worried lest he did something wrong.

He had thought about going to speak with Trina directly. He wanted to invite her on a picnic or for a walk by the creek. But to do so directly seemed wrong. He did not know how she felt about him, or if she had only been nice for the sake of her aunt. Elmer had little experience with women. He always got nervous and backed off before anything could happen. But this time, he was resolved to discover if his own burgeoning feelings might be reciprocated.

He had decided to take Starlight with him on a visit to Trina's *mamm's* house. He knew how much she liked horses and he intended to offer her the chance to come riding with him that very day. The horse would provide a talking point, and Elmer would show Trina just how good a rider he was.

He had the route planned out in his head. They would ride up onto the ridge and take in the views across

Faith's Creek below. He had packed some food into the saddle bag – chocolate, apples, and two iced buns from Katy Zook's bakery stall in the market.

"If this doesn't work, I don't know what will," he said to himself, leading Starlight out of the paddock next to the house belonging to his *mamm* and *daed* and down the lane in the direction of Trina's house.

As he approached, Elmer's nerves grew worse. What if she did not want to go riding with him? What if she told him it was a foolish idea and he was being silly? Self-doubt overcame him and he paused, wondering whether to turn back.

"Why would she do that? She's a nice person. Just... take a risk," he said out loud, cursing himself for his lack of resolve.

Other men managed perfectly well to talk to women, but not Elmer. He just got nervous and fled. But today would be different, and taking a deep breath, he walked on, tethering Starlight to a post outside the house. There was no sign of Trina, but Elmer could see her brother – whose name he thought was Noah – sitting on the front porch. He was whittling something with a knife, and he looked up as Elmer approached.

"Did my aunt send you?" Noah asked.

Elmer shook his head. "It's Noah, isn't it? I was looking for your sister. Is she around?" he asked, stuffing his hands in his pockets lest the boy could see he was trembling.

Noah put down the piece of wood he was whittling and shook his head.

"*Nee*, she's working. She's always working," he replied.

Elmer had not been prepared for this. He had convinced himself Trina would be at home waiting. He would ask her to ride with him and she would agree. They would ride up onto the ridge and eat the iced buns together before returning home. This was not how it was meant to be.

"Oh... right. I didn't realize," he said, uncertain of what to do next.

"She's there every morning and late into the afternoon. Sometimes, she stays there until the evening," Noah continued.

"At the professor's house? The *Englischer*?" Elmer asked.

Trina's aunt had spoken to him about Trina's new employment. She was not happy with her niece for taking a job with an outsider. Elmer had not understood her objection. The talk around Faith's Creek was that the professor was an eccentric sort, recently retired from Harvard. Elmer could not see why Trina should not work for him, even if it meant his own disappointment at her not being at home.

"That's right. She's always there," he replied.

"Don't you think that's *gut*? She's got a job, and she's obviously *gut* at it," Elmer asked, thinking he should say something in Trina's defense.

Noah shook his head. "She shouldn't be working for an *Englischer*. That's what my Aunt Leah says," he said.

Elmer could hear Leah saying as much. It was a strange attitude and one that had overtaken her nephew, too.

"We shouldn't judge people before we know them. I'm sure this professor is a *gut* sort. Perhaps if you meet him..." Elmer began, but Noah interrupted him.

"He's got a son, too. That's what Trina says. She's always talking about him. He's going to come back to Faith's Creek and take care of his *daed*. Trina's going to arrange it. She wants to meet him," Noah said.

At these words, Elmer's heart sank.

He had spoken of not judging others, but his heart now betrayed him as a searing sense of jealousy went through him.

"A son? I thought he was a bachelor," Elmer said.

Noah shook his head.

"I don't know. It's just what I heard Trina saying. She wants the professor's son to come to Faith's Creek," he said.

Elmer's heart sank even more.

He had made a fool of himself – that much was certain. He had been naïve to think his encounter with Trina at the cookout had been anything more than a duty on her part. Trina's aunt had spoken of making a "special intro-duction," but all the while, Trina had been thinking of someone else. How could Elmer compete with the son of a Harvard professor? This man was probably a doctor or a lawyer or a banker – he would be wealthy, with *gut* prospects, and a smile to match. Elmer sighed.

"I see," he said.

Noah looked at him curiously. "Do you want me to tell Trina you came by?" he asked.

Elmer shook his head. "It's all right. I wanted to surprise her by introducing her to Starlight – that's my horse. He's tethered up by the gate. But I'll catch her another time," he replied, even as he knew there would not be another time.

It had taken all Elmer's courage to overcome his nerves at the prospect of speaking with Trina on his own terms. It had been all worked out, but now his plans were ruined, and he felt embarrassed for his eagerness. He should have realized Trina was only being polite, and he thanked Noah for his time and left in a state of dejection.

"It's always the same. It always goes wrong," he said to himself, sighing as he untethered Starlight and made his way slowly back to the smallholding.

Trina's aunt would not be pleased – first, working for an *Englischer* and now, wishing to court one. Elmer shook his head, knowing it would be a long time before he ever plucked up the courage to do this again...

CHAPTER EIGHT

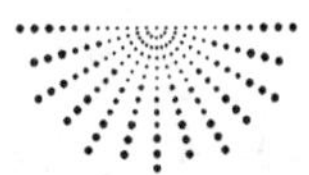

The professor was coughing. Trina stood outside the door of his study, listening to the rasps coming from inside. Doctor Yoder had called again that morning, and the prognosis was not good. Professor Lindorp had emphysema. His cough was a symptom of it, along with breathlessness and fatigue. Treatment would help, but the condition was there to stay, and the professor was under strict orders not to exert himself.

"I'm all right, Doctor," he had said, but Doctor Yoder thought otherwise.

"Make sure he rests. I don't want this getting any worse," he had told Trina, after explaining how to help the professor during a bout of coughing.

There were medicines to take, and the professor had also been advised to lose weight.

"Which means no more apple fritters, I'm afraid, and less butter on those buttered noodles," he had told Trina at lunchtime.

Trina was worried. She had noticed the professor's deterioration even in the past few weeks and she wondered if he would really take the diagnosis seriously. She knocked at the study door and opened it. The professor was sitting in his usual chair with a book open on his lap, and he looked up and shook his head.

"I'll bring the house down with this cough," he said.

Trina looked at him with a worried expression on her face. "I'll top your water jug up," she replied.

She went to the kitchen and filled the jug, returning to the study a moment later. The professor did not look well. His face had turned suddenly pale, and he had pulled a blanket around his shoulders.

"There's quite a chill in the air, isn't there?" he said.

Trina glanced out of the window in surprise. Her look was greeted with bright sunshine, and Trina herself had spent the best part of the day trying to keep cool.

"Should I go and fetch Doctor Yoder again?" she asked.

The professor shook his head. "I don't like bothering him. Just bring me another blanket from upstairs, if you will."

"What about your son? Shouldn't he know what's happened? He wouldn't want to think you were sick and that he didn't know," Trina said.

At the mention of his son, the professor turned his face away. "He wouldn't be interested. Dominic wouldn't want me disturbing him. He only cares about his work," he said.

Trina did not think it was her place to argue.

But as she went upstairs to fetch the blanket, she could not help thinking how sad it was for the professor and his son to remain estranged. She imagined how she would feel if her *mamm* was ill and Noah kept it from her.

"I'll write to him," she said to herself, pausing on the landing outside the professor's den.

It was here he watched old western films on a battered television perched on a stand in the corner – they were his favorites – and he wrote his personal correspondence. Trina had seen his address book lying open the previous day when she had come to dust, and now she slipped into the room, her heart beating fast as she flicked through the pages.

"Klosh, Kopperton, Kraut... Lander, Levison, Lindorp... Dominic Lindorp, Lindorp and Cooper, 191 Setterburg Street, Philadelphia, Pennsylvania, 63458," she whispered, memorizing the address before returning the address book to its open place on the desk.

She fetched a blanket and returned downstairs, finding the professor with his eyes closed, his face pale, his breathing labored.

"Thank you," he said, as Trina tucked the blanket over him.

"Just call out if you need me. I'll be in the kitchen," Trina said, repeating the address over to herself in her mind.

Back in the kitchen, she wrote it down and began to compose a letter. In it, she introduced herself and wrote of her concern for Professor Lindorp. She urged Dominic to visit his *daed,* even as she knew doing so would mean the professor discovering she had interfered in his affairs. But some things were more important than a scolding, and if she was able to reunite the two men, then something *gut* would have come out of her going behind the professor's back. As she sealed the letter, Trina offered up a prayer, asking *Gott* to bless her endeavors.

"I'm doing the right thing," she told herself, as Professor Lindorp called out for a glass of water.

Having written the letter, Trina was in two minds if to send it. She thought about how she would feel if it were her *daed* lying coughing and spluttering each day. The professor's condition was getting worse, and Trina knew time was of the essence. Doctor Yoder had provided treatment, but conditions like this could easily take a turn for the worst, and when winter came – and it came hard in Faith's Creek – the danger of pneumonia loomed.

She did not tell her *mamm* – or anyone – of her intentions. Her *mamm* would only worry about what her aunt would say if it was discovered Trina was interfering in an *Englischer's affairs*, and besides, she may receive no response from the lawyer, whom Professor Lindorp always described as being exceedingly busy.

It was two days after she had written it that Trina posted the letter to Dominic's office. She said a prayer and put it in the mailbox at the end of the lane near her house. The deed was done, for good or ill.

"He might not even reply," she told herself, but that did not stop her from enquiring of her *mamm* and Noah each day on her arrival back from Professor Lindorp's house.

"Who'd be writing to you? It's not like you've got any secret admirers, or maybe one..." Noah taunted her, but Trina was not in the mood for mischief-making.

"Oh, do be quiet, Noah. You're just being silly. I wrote to a friend, that's all," she said, even as her *mamm* looked at her curiously.

It was two weeks later, and Trina had all but given up on Dominic Lindorp ever writing back to her. She was disappointed in him, but perhaps her aunt was right – the ways of *Englischers* were different from those of her own community. The professor's son was a lawyer with responsibilities, and perhaps he really did put those ahead of his own family. She was ready to forget the whole affair. She had tried her best and done what she believed to be right. If the professor's son wanted nothing to do with his *daed*, then so be it.

"There's a letter for you, Trina. Postmarked Philadelphia," her *mamm* said, as Trina came up the steps that afternoon.

Trina's eyes grew wide with astonishment, even as she tried to hide it from her *mamm*, who was holding the letter in her hands.

"Is that so? Oh, I guess it's from... Barbara," she said, saying the first name that came into her mind.

"You don't know anyone called Barbara," her *mamm* replied, but Trina had already snatched the letter from her *mamm's* hand and ran into the house with it.

With trembling hands, Trina opened it. It was written on headed notepaper, from no less than the offices of Lindorp and Cooper.

"Dear Trina, thank you for your letter... so forth... I knew nothing about my father's ill-health... I'll be arriving in Faith's Creek..."

"Tomorrow!" Trina exclaimed, her eyes wide with astonishment and her heart skipping a beat.

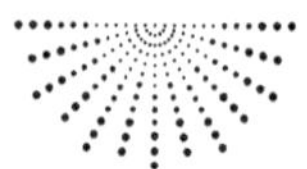

CHAPTER NINE

"Of course, you can come. I want you here," Leah Speicher said, even as Elmer looked nervous.

It had been Leah's idea for him to come for cake and coffee at the house. He had been working on the smallholding all morning, and his employer had come to inform him that her sister, her niece, and her nephew would be calling on them that afternoon. She had suggested Elmer join them, but after the disaster of his previous attempt at courtship, Elmer was unsure.

"I don't want to get in the way. You're family. Won't you want to talk about family things?" he asked, but it seemed Leah had already made up her mind.

"Trina's going to be there. The two of you got on so well at the cookout, I thought you'd jump at the chance of seeing her again," Leah retorted.

Elmer did not want to upset her. He liked working for the Speichers, but he did not want to admit he had already tried and failed, to see Trina again. The thought of meeting her under such circumstances, of hearing her pretend once more to show interest in him... he blushed at the thought, even as it seemed he had no choice but to follow Leah's lead.

"Well... that's very kind of you," he said.

Leah smiled. "I've made a seed cake, and there're buns and chocolate biscuits. Get yourself washed up at two o'clock and come into the house," she replied.

Before Elmer could think of any reason to object, she had hurried off.

He sighed, returning to the vegetable patch and shaking his head. The thought of seeing Trina filled him with anxiety. What would he say to her? He wondered if Noah had told her about his arrival with the horse... how embarrassing. He concentrated on the weeding, listening out for the sound of the grandfather clock in the parlor – the window was open, and he could hear its chimes drifting across the garden. When two o'clock came, Elmer dusted himself off and hurried into the shed where there was a tap, splashing water on his face and hands and hoping he looked presentable.

"Not that it matters. She's got her man from Philadelphia," he said to himself, hoping the ordeal would be over as soon as possible.

He made his way across the garden, through the orchard, and up the steps onto the porch. He could hear voices through the open parlor window, and he knocked, taking a deep breath as Leah opened the door.

"Oh, Elmer, we were just talking about you," she said, ushering him inside as though the entire thing was a coincidence.

Inside, Elmer found Trina, her *mamm*, and her brother, sitting at the table. A white cloth had been spread over it, and the best china was laid out. The seed cake was in pride of place, and Leah ushered Elmer to a seat next to Trina, much to his embarrassment. She was looking ever so pretty, dressed in a blue dress and white *kapp*. A lock of blonde hair was creeping from beneath her *kapp*, and her pretty blue eyes gazed up at him with a smile.

"It's nice to see you, Elmer. You've still not brought the horse to see me," Trina said, smiling at Elmer, who blushed.

"Oh, well... you see..." he began.

Leah interrupted him. "There'll be plenty of time for that, I'm sure," she said, handing around a plate of biscuits.

Elmer felt thoroughly out of place. The others talked about family matters – matters Elmer knew nothing of. But he could not help but notice the way Trina appeared distracted. She kept glancing at the clock, and every time it chimed a quarter, she seemed to grow more fidgety.

"Are you enjoying working for Leah, Elmer?" Rebecca, Trina's *mamm* asked, and Elmer nodded.

"Oh... *jah*, I am, *denke*. I just hope I'm doing a *gut* job," he said.

Leah laughed. "You're doing an excellent job, Elmer. I wouldn't have invited you in for tea if I didn't think that," she said, offering him another slice of seed cake.

But Elmer knew her motivation well enough, and he was worried about what would happen when she was disabused of the notion that her niece and Elmer might begin a courtship. She would not be pleased to hear he had failed to dissuade her from the charms of an *Englischer*. The clock now struck half-past three, and Trina leaped to her feet in a sudden burst of excitement. The others looked at her in surprise.

"Trina, what's wrong?" Rebecca asked as Trina snatched up her shawl.

"I've got to go. I've got to be somewhere," she exclaimed, even as her *mamm* tutted.

"Trina... your aunt asked you here for tea. It's rude to leave so suddenly," she said, but Trina was already putting on her cape.

She glanced back at the table, catching Elmer's eye as she did so.

"I'm sorry. I promised the professor I'd run an errand for him this afternoon," she said, and now her aunt rolled her eyes.

"I see. This is for the *Englischer*. I don't know what's come over you, Trina. You've become obsessed with that man. Why can't you stick with your own kind instead of chasing after outsiders?" she demanded.

But Trina made no reply, and before any further objections could be made, she had left the house, banging the door behind her. Leah shook her head, glancing at Elmer, who felt thoroughly embarrassed.

"I don't know what's gotten into her. I'm sorry about that, Leah, really, I am," Rebecca said, but Leah waved her hand dismissively.

"It doesn't matter. But you need to go after her, Elmer," she said, pointing towards the door.

"Me?" Elmer exclaimed for he had not expected Leah to suggest such a thing.

"*Jah*, you. Go after her and make her see sense," she exclaimed.

Elmer was uncertain how he could ever make a woman like Trina change her mind. She was strong-willed, determined, stubborn, even – all qualities Elmer lacked. He was a gentle sort who shied away from conflict, the sort for whom chasing after others was the very last thing he wanted to do.

"But I..." Elmer began, even as Leah seized his hat and virtually pushed him out of the door.

"We can't let her become involved with these *Englis-chers*. That's how we lost our identity as a community," she said, pointing after Trina, whose figure could be seen disappearing along the lane.

Elmer sighed. He felt like a fool to be doing this, and he was certain Trina would think him so. What would he say to her? What would she say to him? Reluctantly, he followed her, keeping some distance behind, and knew if she turned around, he would have a lot of explaining to do.

"Why can't anything be simple?" he asked himself.

To his surprise, Trina was not heading in the direction of Forest Hill. She turned at the end of the lane, heading instead for the Greyhound bus stop. Elmer followed, his curiosity peaked. Trina had said nothing about leaving Faith's Creek, and Elmer was at a loss to know what to do. Was she running away? He could not let her do so.

"But I can't stop her," he told himself, shaking his head as he hid behind a gate, watching Trina, who was now waiting at the bus stop.

A few moments later, the bus came into sight. It was one of those from the city, the sort that treks across the state, covering vast distances, and stopping at just about every place imaginable. Elmer had taken one to Philadelphia on his *rumspringa*, and now it pulled up, the doors sighing open to reveal a tall man with black hair, smartly dressed in a suit and tie. He looked quite out of place for Faith's Creek, and to Elmer's amazement, Trina went hurrying up to him. Elmer was too far away to hear what they were saying, but there was no doubt the man was grateful to see her - happy, even.

"Of course... it's the professor's son," Elmer thought to himself, remembering Noah's words, even as the thought made him feel terribly sad indeed.

It all made sense now. Trina had been waiting to meet the professor's son off the bus. They had probably been corresponding for weeks – or even talking on the telephone. Elmer knew the professor's house was equipped with a telephone, and now he realized all his hopes were gone. How could he possibly compete with a man like that? He sighed and sat back in the long grass at the edge of the field, watching through the gate as Trina and the professor's son hurried past. There was no point in following them any longer. Elmer had seen enough.

"Just forget about her," he told himself, even as he was filled with sadness at the possibility of what might have been.

CHAPTER TEN

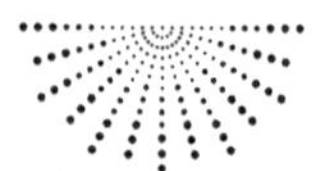

"How was your journey?" Trina asked as she met Dominic off the Greyhound bus.

He was taller than she had imagined him to be, with black hair and green eyes, which flashed a smile as he greeted her. He was dressed smartly in a black suit and red tie and carried a leather suitcase with him – making him look quite out of place amongst the other people getting off at the Faith's Creek stop.

"I haven't been on one of these in years. I'd forgotten the suspension is non-existent." He gave her another smile. "However, it's good to meet you, Trina. I must say, I'm glad you wrote to me. I had no idea he was so unwell. He's too stubborn to tell me, and he thinks all that business with our disagreement... oh, I know I've not always been the best son, but if he'd not told me..." he said, shaking his head.

It was clear to Trina that the arrival of her letter had caused quite a stir in Dominic. He looked worried, even as he thanked her again for having written to him.

"I didn't tell your *daed* that I wrote to you. I hope he's not going to be angry with me for doing so. It's just... I thought about how I'd feel if someone kept an illness in the family from me. I'd be terribly upset, I know that for certain," she said, still having to justify to herself the fact that she went behind Professor Lindorp's back.

"My pa and I are too alike. We're both stubborn as mules. He had his way. I had mine. We're like two peas in a pod, except the pod isn't big enough for the both of us. When he moved all the way out here... it just wasn't so easy to keep a check on him – not that he'd have wanted me to keep a check on him anyway. It seems a nice place, though – even if it is in the back of beyond," Dominic replied as he looked around. The expression on his face was a little stunned -- as if he had never seen such a place before.

Trina led him along the lane, pointing out the things they could see. Forest Hill stood prominently before them. It was opposite the ridge, wooded, and with the professor's house nestled amongst the trees.

"A lot of people were suspicious of your *daed* when he first arrived. Oh, by the way, I'm sorry if the way I say certain words sounds odd. It's just our way of speaking," Trina said, suddenly realizing that the language of the community might have seemed archaic to an outsider from the city.

"Not at all. I grew up hearing my pa – my *daed* – talking in all sorts of dialects. He was interested in the way the early settlers spoke. It wasn't all English – far from it," Dominic replied.

Trina liked Dominic. Their lives could not have been more different, but he seemed entirely easygoing, laid back, and grateful to her for informing him of his *daed's* ailment. They talked all the way to the front gate of the professor's house, pausing on the porch as Trina glanced at Dominic nervously.

"I left his dinner in the kitchen. He's not expecting me back today. He might be asleep – he's been sleeping a lot in his chair lately. We should knock," Trina said, not wanting to let herself in and startle the professor with the arrival of the son he was not expecting.

She knocked at the door and waited. A moments later, footsteps could be heard in the hall and the door was opened. The professor looked weary, his face was pale, and his shoulders hunched over. But at the sight of Dominic, he stared in amazement, looking from him to Trina and back and shaking his head.

"Hello, Pa," Dominic said.

Professor Lindorp shook his head and rubbed his eyes.

"Am I dreaming? What are you doing here?" he asked, a note of suspicion entering his voice.

"Please... Professor Lindorp. I wrote to Dominic. I was worried about you. You've been getting worse these past few weeks, and I thought he'd want to know," Trina replied.

She half expected the professor to sack her on the spot. But she was convinced she had done the right thing in telling Dominic the truth, and if it meant losing her job, then so be it.

A look of anger came over his face.

"I told you not to disturb him. I told you, I'm not ill, I'm..." he began, but his words were interrupted by a violent bout of coughing, his shoulder hunched over as he steadied himself on the door frame.

Now, it was Dominic who stepped forward.

"I'm glad she did, Pa. Didn't you think I'd want to know you were ill? That silly disagreement we had over Uncle Paul's will. It came to nothing. The house went to Elsie. It's done with now. I don't care about the money. But I do care about you. You moved down here away from everyone who cared about you. You're lucky to have someone like Trina. She was worried about you, and she wrote to tell me. That's all. I came straightaway," he said.

Trina was grateful to him for defending her.

She knew she had done the right thing, even if the professor still looked somewhat angry at her for doing so.

"Straightaway?" Professor Lindorp asked.

"Straightaway. Trina's letter got lost in the office mail. I opened it two days ago and made an immediate reply. Lindy's worried, too. She's going to come down here just as soon as the City Vs Vian case is over. She's been working really hard on it. You'll enjoy hearing about it when she gets here. But can I come in? I've had a long journey and I could do with something to eat," Dominic said.

Trina was confused. She did not know who Lindy was, even as she speculated it might be Dominic's wife. She knew nothing about him, save he was Professor Lindorp's son and a lawyer in Philadelphia. Professor Lindorp sighed.

"I'm sorry, Trina. I'm not very good at letting other people manage me. It makes me feel as though I'm losing control. But... you were right to tell Dominic the truth. I was a fool to keep it from him. I thought I could manage. But I'm not sure I can. I've missed you, Dominic," he said, smiling weakly at his son, who put his bag down and stepped forward to embrace his *daed*. As he pulled back the professor had tears in his eyes.

Trina welled up, too.

"I've missed you, too, Pa. I'm sorry if I've been distant. We're both as bad as one another. Too stubborn for our own good. Lindy kept telling me to call you. But when Trina's letter arrived, I realized I didn't even have a number for you down here," Dominic said.

"I got rid of the phone. It was making poor Trina jump every time it rang. Come in, we'll have some... coffee," Professor Lindorp said, smiling at Trina, who gave a sigh of relief.

"I'll make up one of the spare rooms, then we'll see about something to eat. You two go and sit down. You've got a lot of catching up to do," she said, thankful that everything had worked out for the best.

Soon, a spare room was made up, and Trina was busy cooking buttered noodles and apple fritters at the request of Professor Lindorp.

"You wait until you taste these, Dominic. You'll forget all about McDonald's and Wendy's – or any of those fancy restaurants you lawyers eat in," he had said, smiling at Trina, who had blushed.

"This is delicious," Dominic said, after taking a forkful of buttered noodles.

"It's an Amish recipe of my *mamm's*. It's all in the seasoning, that's what she always says," Trina said, smiling at the sight of the two men tucking into her food.

"Do you think Lindy's going to like it here?" Professor Lindorp said, tucking into his own plate of noodles as Dominic wiped his mouth with a napkin.

"Oh, I'm sorry, Trina, I should've told you – Lindy's my fiancée. She's a lawyer in her own firm in Philadelphia – she is much more prestigious than me. We met at

Cornell. I wasn't going anywhere near Harvard – not with my pa teaching there," Dominic said.

Professor Lindorp laughed. It made him look so much better and he even had a touch of color in his cheeks.

"And I wouldn't have wanted him there, either. A person has to make their own way in life. That's what I say. I was glad when Dominic got his place at Cornell, and I'm glad to be seeing Lindy again. She's a remarkable young lady. I think you and her might get on well, Trina," he said.

Trina was not sure what she would have in common with a Cornell-educated lawyer from Philadelphia, but she was only too glad to have done what she could to bring Professor Lindorp and his son back together. She cleared away the meal and left out a simple supper on the kitchen table.

"I'm really very grateful to you, Trina," Dominic said, catching her in the hallway just as she was putting on her shawl to leave.

"Oh, you don't have to thank me. I'm just glad your *daed* didn't get mad at me – not too much, at least," she replied, smiling at him as he laughed.

"He wouldn't – he just doesn't always recognize what he needs. And neither do I. You brought us back together, and I'll always be grateful for that. I'd also be grateful if you'd continue your job as the housekeeper here. When Lindy comes, there'll be three of us, and none of us are very practically minded," he said.

"Are you planning on staying in Faith's Creek?" Trina asked.

Dominic nodded.

"The world's shrinking. We can work anywhere, and already, I rather like it here," he replied...

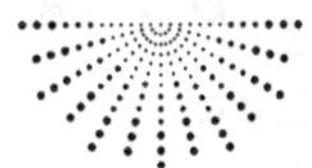

CHAPTER ELEVEN

The next day, Trina returned to the house on Forest Hill bright and early. She wanted to make breakfast for the professor and his son, even though she found the house quiet at the early hour she arrived.

She had mastered the kitchen and its various appliances now, and she set about making pancakes, feeling certain that a lawyer from Philadelphia would enjoy a stack of homemade pancakes.

It turned out that Dominic Lindorp *was* partial to pancakes, and a little later that morning, he applauded Trina on her cookery skills, having devoured a stack of them with maple syrup and blueberries.

"Delicious. Absolutely delicious," he exclaimed, laying down his knife and fork.

Professor Lindorp had only managed two with butter and salt, but he, too, pronounced them delicious, and Trina was pleased. She liked having people to cook for, and now she hurried upstairs to make the beds and air out the rooms as Dominic and his *daed* sat talking at the table. The professor's mood had certainly improved, and some color had returned to his face, much to Trina's relief. As she came back downstairs, Dominic emerged from the dining room to meet her.

"Can I get you some more coffee?" she asked, but he shook his head.

"No. Thank you, but I was wondering... would you be willing to give me a tour of Faith's Creek? If I'm going to stick around for a while, I'd like to know where I'm going and what's the best way here and there," he said.

Trina nodded. She would be only too happy to give him a tour of Faith's Creek. She had lived there all her life, and knew every path, every lane, every road, every house, and just about every person.

"I'd be delighted. It's a lovely place – especially down by the creek. I'll just get my shawl and we can go. I've already put a casserole on the stove for lunch," she said, smiling at Dominic, who nodded.

"I'm in your hands," he replied.

Outside, the day was turning warm. The sky was bright blue, and a gentle breeze was blowing across the cornfields. It was a perfect day for a walk around Faith's Creek, and they set off together, talking happily as they went.

Trina found Dominic more than easy to get along with, and they walked together by the creek, through the woods, and up onto the ridge, making a loop that brought them down towards her aunt's smallholding.

"My aunt and uncle live here. They own the smallholding, and there's an orchard, too. They employ a couple of laborers. I'll introduce you to one. He's called Elmer. He's really nice," Trina said, opening the gate and ushering Dominic up the path.

She felt she owed Elmer an explanation. She had enjoyed seeing him the day before, even if she had made the conversation feel somewhat awkward owing to her agitation at watching the clock for Dominic's arrival. She wanted to apologize to Elmer and explain the reason for her agitation. He was working in the vegetable patch, pulling up weeds by the potatoes, and Trina called to him, beckoning Dominic to follow.

"Trina?" Elmer said, tossing aside a large weed he had just pulled up.

"I want you to meet someone. This is Dominic. He's Professor Lindorp's son. He's a lawyer from Philadelphia, but he's going to be staying here awhile," she said.

Elmer dusted the dirt off his hands. He looked somewhat embarrassed, straightening himself up and holding out his hand.

"I'm pleased to meet you, I'm sure," he said, as Dominic took his hand and shook it.

"Likewise. You've got quite a crop here. I'd be grateful for any advice on growing you can give me. My pa's got a huge garden up there on Forest Hill. I was thinking we might dig a vegetable patch and grow our own food. I'm sure you could come up with some delicious recipes for whatever we grew, Trina," he said, turning to Trina, who nodded.

"Oh, certainly. I'd love to help. You could help, too, Elmer," she said, trying to encourage him.

She had been sad that Elmer had not pursued his offer of introducing her to Starlight. She liked him far more than she had expected, even as it pained her to admit her aunt had been right. He was kind, thoughtful, and pleasant to be around, even if he did suffer from a crippling shyness.

"Well... you could start with beets and leeks. They're easy," Elmer said, glancing shyly at Trina, who smiled.

"We'll start with them, then. Perhaps my aunt would let me have some of the seedlings from the hothouse. That's where you start them, isn't it?" Trina asked, and Elmer nodded.

"We start everything in there. I've got some flowers that just bloomed from seedlings. I'll show you," he said, and he hurried off, still with that same nervous expression on his face.

"He seems a good sort," Dominic said.

Trina nodded. "He's a *gut* man. He's offered to show me his horse – I hope he does," she replied, just as Elmer came hurrying back.

He was carrying a beautiful bloom in his hand – a peach-colored rose with delicate petals and a sweet fragrance – which he now held out to her, a blush coming over his face.

"I picked it for you. I'm glad you'll be happy now," he said, glancing at Dominic.

Trina was confused as to what he meant, but the rose was beautiful, and she took it from him and smiled.

"That's very kind, Elmer, *denke*," she said, flattered he should think of such a gesture.

"I hear you ride, Elmer," Dominic said.

Elmer nodded. "A little," he said.

Trina laughed. "A little? You're one of the best horsemen in Faith's Creek – that's what everyone says. Not that I've met Starlight yet," she said, raising her eyebrows at Elmer, who now turned a deep shade of red.

"I just... haven't got around to it," he replied.

Trina could not understand why he appeared so nervous. Perhaps Dominic unnerved him, and she thought it best now to say their goodbyes.

"I'll see you in the next few days," she said, bringing the rose to her nose and breathing in its sweet aroma.

Elmer nodded and gave a weak smile.

"All right..." he said, glancing at Dominic, who smiled.

"I'm glad to meet you, Elmer. Call at my pa's place anytime. We'd be glad to see you – and hear more about planting out a vegetable garden," he said.

Trina led Dominic back across the garden. She was pleased they had not encountered her aunt or uncle. She could well imagine what they would say about another *Englischer* arriving in Faith's Creek, even one with Dominic's credentials.

"I'm sorry. I don't know what came over Elmer," Trina said after they were out of earshot.

Dominic only smiled.

"I deal with all sorts of people in my daily life. He was just a little nervous about meeting someone new. That's all," he replied, but Trina was confused.

The rose, Elmer's comment about her having what she wanted, and the way he had looked at her... it was all very strange.

"I hope I haven't upset him," she said to herself, as they made their way towards the home of Bishop Beiler, whom Trina was certain would be pleased to welcome Faith's Creek's newest resident.

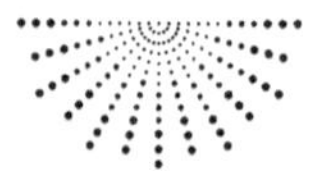

"I'm just not happy about it, Trina. You're becoming more *Englisch* by the day," Leah said, folding her arms and looking at Trina with a disdainful gaze.

Trina knew her aunt could not offer a more devastating insult than this. To her aunt, identity meant everything. She was Amish through and through. She had not even left Faith's Creek on her own *rumspringa* and knew nothing of the world beyond the confines of the cornfields. The outside world did not concern her, nor did she wish to be enlightened so that it might.

As much as she loved her, Trina had always thought her narrowminded, a contrast to her own *mamm* who, whilst always respecting tradition, had raised Trina with a healthy interest in things beyond the limits of the community. To be accused of being an *Englischer* was to be accused of betraying everything her aunt believed in.

"It's a job, Aunt Leah. I need a job and it's a *gut* job. They're kind people," Trina replied.

She was carrying a bag of books the professor had lent her – books on Amish history and the first settlers – and now she set them down on the table on the porch. Her aunt grimaced.

"What are these?" she asked.

Trina sighed. "They're books the professor lent me. They're about our ancestors. If you'd bothered to ask, you'd have known Professor Lindorp is an expert in Amish history and the early settlers. And his son..." she began, but now her aunt interrupted her, even as her *mamm* looked on in silence.

"Oh, yes, the son... now we come to the matter in hand," Leah replied.

Trina had wondered why her aunt had been waiting for her on her return from work that afternoon. She and Trina's *mamm* were drinking lemonade on the porch, and now she folded her arms and fixed Trina with an even more disdainful look.

"The matter in hand? Dominic's come from Philadelphia to look after his *daed*. The professor's not well, you know that. Don't you think a son should do that? Isn't that one of our values – family?" Trina exclaimed.

"It's not the only thing he's come here for though, is it?" Leah asked, raising her eyebrows.

Trina was at a loss for words. She had not expected this onslaught, and now she looked to her *mamm*, who shook her head.

"Really, Leah... there's no need for that," Rebecca replied, but her aunt was on the warpath.

"He's not a suitable match. I won't have my niece chasing after an *Englischer*. I don't care if he's got money... if he's a lawyer, or whatever – no way!" she exclaimed, and she banged her fist down hard on the table so that the jug of lemonade and the glasses shook.

Trina stared at her in astonishment. She had never thought of Dominic as anything more than a friend. Besides, he was engaged to Lindy, and there was no question of impropriety on his part. He had behaved entirely as a gentleman, and Trina was shocked her aunt should even suggest such a thing.

"But, I'm not..." she protested, even as her aunt interrupted.

"And poor Elmer. You've embarrassed the boy. He made all that effort with you at the cookout and tried to be nice to you over coffee and cake. He wanted to show you his horse, but no, you were off at the professor's house – Noah told me he looked devastated when he came here and you weren't to be found," her aunt said.

Trina's eyes grew wide with astonishment. Noah had not told her about the horse... and to think she had accused Elmer of not bringing Starlight to meet her. She faltered, realizing that if her aunt had made such an assumption, others must surely have done so, too.

"I... you've got it wrong, but I'm sorry Elmer's upset," Trina said, feeling her stomach twist as she spoke.

It was no wonder Elmer had looked embarrassed when she had introduced Dominic to him. The rose, his words... it all made sense now.

"Oh, really? And perhaps you'd like to tell me how I've got it wrong," her aunt replied.

"Dominic's betrothed to be married. His fiancée's coming from Philadelphia soon. She's a lawyer, too. They're going to stay with the professor. He needs looking after. But I was only being friendly to Dominic. We weren't courting or anything. He's got lots of female friends – he told me. It's not unusual. We get on and I've helped him look after his *daed*. That's all. I don't see anything more than that," she said, and now it was her aunt's turn to look surprised.

"Fiancée? He's going to be married? But I thought..." she began, and now it was Rebecca who interrupted.

"Perhaps we didn't think enough, Leah," she said, and Trina's aunt sighed.

"All right, I admit it. I jumped the gun. But that doesn't mean there isn't a laborer on my smallholding who's chewed up about a certain young woman," she said, raising her eyebrows at Trina once again.

Trina *did* feel guilty. She had not meant to confuse Elmer. She liked him. She really liked him, and now she realized he liked her, too, she wanted to set things straight. Trina had been too busy with other matters to think much about her own feelings. She had pushed them aside, unwilling to admit her own desires – the desire for love, a husband, a family. But that was what she wanted, and in introducing her to Elmer, her aunt had sown a seed, one which could still blossom, if given the right tending. She realized she had been foolish not to think how it might have looked for her to be so friendly with Dominic. People in Faith's Creek were already suspicious of the professor, and it would not have taken much for them, too, to have drawn their own foolish conclusions.

"I didn't realize he brought the horse here. I didn't realize how he felt," Trina said.

Leah shook her head. "Didn't I try my hardest to set things up between you? The cookout, inviting him for coffee and cake, extolling your virtues to him – all for nothing!" she exclaimed.

Trina shook her head. "It wasn't all for nothing. I like him. He's nice. He's shy, but I understand why. I'm glad you introduced us, and I'll go and find him and tell him as much," she said.

Her mind was made up. She would find Elmer and see if the two of them might start again. There were things she needed to make clear – not least the nature of her relationship with Dominic. She still had the rose in a vase in her bedroom, and now she hurried inside, smiling at the sight of it as she changed out of her work clothes and into a clean blue dress, glancing at herself in the mirror and sighing.

"You can make things right," she told herself, as she headed in the direction of her aunt's smallholding, determined to tell Elmer the truth.

CHAPTER THIRTEEN

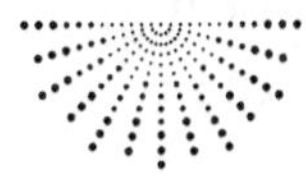

$\mathcal{E}$lmer was miserable. He had the afternoon off and was brushing down Starlight in the paddock next to the home of his parents. Horses were far easier than people, he had decided.

"Don't you think so, Starlight?" he said, voicing his thoughts out loud.

The horse whinnied and shook its mane. Elmer smiled and rested his head on the horse's neck, running his hand along its back. The talk of Faith's Creek was that Trina was courting the *Englischer,* and Elmer had no reason to disbelieve it. He had seen the two of them together, and the thought of presenting Trina with a rose now made him cringe.

"He must have thought I was pathetic," he said to himself, sighing, even as his feelings for Trina remained the same.

He was in love with her, but it was a love he knew would never be reciprocated. A laborer on a smallholding could never compete with a slick city lawyer from Philadelphia. Dominic and Trina would not remain in Faith's Creek for long. They would get married and move away, and Elmer would be left miserable. He saw no other future for himself, lost in the depths of despair.

"It just wasn't to be," he told himself, but try as he might, Elmer could not lift himself out of his depression.

He had allowed his imagination to run away with him. He had pictured marriage, *kinner*, a home of their own. Elmer was skilled with his hands, and he wanted to do something practical to make a living. Mending buggies was the obvious answer, and he intended to settle down and start his own business, just as soon as he could save enough money from his work on the smallholding. But such dreams seemed as nothing now there was no one with whom to share them.

He patted Starlight, raising his head from the horse's neck, and rummaging in his pocket for a sugar lump. He would get over it in time, but for now, there was no doubting his misery.

"We'll stick together though, won't we?" he said, and the horse whinnied.

But at that moment, Elmer was surprised at the sound of footsteps hurrying toward him, and he looked up to find Trina standing by the gate. He stared at her in surprise. What did she want? Why had she come here? His hands began to tremble, and he did not know what to say, fearful of making a fool of himself.

"Elmer? Can I talk to you?" she asked, smiling at him.

Elmer nodded. He could not think what she was going to say to him. Would she embarrass him? His cheeks flushed red, and he swallowed hard.

"Yes..." he said.

Trina climbed over the gate into the paddock. "I'm glad I get to meet Starlight at last," she said, reaching out to pat the horse's nose.

"He's just had a brush down. I might take him out to ride later on," Elmer replied.

Trina nodded. "Perhaps I could come along, too," she said.

Elmer's eyes grew wide with astonishment. "You? I mean... Do you want to come and ride? But..." he began.

Trina reached out and took his hand in hers.

Elmer was shocked. If anyone should see them, there would be a scandal. He pulled away and shook his head.

"Elmer, I think there's been a misunderstanding," Trina said, still smiling at him as she spoke.

Elmer did not understand. It all seemed clear enough to him. The mistake had been his. Trina could marry who she wanted. It was none of his business, even as it hurt him to admit it.

"About what? I don't think so," he replied.

"Listen." Trina shook her head. "A mistake about Dominic. He's engaged to be married," she said.

Elmer's jaw dropped. He stared at Trina in utter disbelief. How could it be so? How could Dominic possibly be betrothed after he had spent so long chasing after Trina?

"But... I don't understand. You and him... he came from Philadelphia. You met him at the Greyhound bus stop," he exclaimed, forgetting Trina did not know he had followed her.

But Trina only shook her head and sighed.

"The professor's ill, Elmer. I wrote to Dominic because I didn't want something to happen to him and for the two of them not to have made their peace. When he arrived, I went to meet him. The day the two of you met, I was showing him around Faith's Creek. He and his fiancée are going to settle here at the house on Forest Hill. I'm sorry if you got the wrong idea, and I'm sorry if I hurt you," she replied.

Elmer drew in a deep breath. He felt a fool for having jumped to so many conclusions, but now a new possibility opened before him. He knew he had to take a chance and overcome his nervousness – this could be his only chance.

"Why did you come to tell me?" he asked, and now it was Trina who blushed.

"Well... I know my aunt tried to set things up between us. I wasn't expecting much from the cookout, but you surprised me. I liked getting to know you, and I was hoping we might carry on getting to know one another better," she replied.

At these words, Elmer's heart almost leaped out of his chest. He could not believe what Trina was saying. It was overwhelming, and he nodded, trembling with excitement at the prospect of what might be.

"I'd like that," he stammered, and she smiled at him – she had the sweetest smile he had ever seen.

"I'm really sorry if I hurt you, Elmer. I didn't mean to. I just didn't think. It was only when my aunt told me what everyone's been saying... I've still got the rose you gave me. I put it in water in a vase on the windowsill in my bedroom. It's so fragrant. I'll press the petals in one of the books Professor Lindorp gave me," she said, causing Elmer to blush further.

He felt so happy he could have jumped for joy. But now he took a deep breath and made a resolve. He would not shy away from his feelings, nor would he let the opportunity pass him by.

"Would you like to go riding tomorrow? I'm sure your aunt wouldn't miss me in the morning. We could take a picnic and ride up onto the ridge. My *mamm* would pack it for us. If you're not too busy, that is?" he said, holding his breath for her reply.

"I'd like that. The professor told me I need to take some time off. I'll pack the picnic for us, and you bring

Starlight over to my house in the morning. I'll be ready about ten o'clock," she said.

Once again, Elmer had to stop himself from letting out a whoop of delight at her words. This was all he had wanted, all he had dreamed of, and now that dream was coming true.

"And you're sure this is what you want?" he asked, fearing even now she might falter.

But Trina shook her head and reached out to take his hand in hers.

"Contrary to what everyone seems to think, I'm not interested in becoming an *Englischer*. I love it here. Faith's Creek's my home, and it always will be. I love working for the professor. He's been kind to me, but that doesn't mean I'm going to start using telephones and watching television – the professor doesn't even have a television, he says it rots the brain. He prefers books," she said.

Elmer laughed. "I shouldn't have jumped to conclusions. I just didn't think I could compete with a slick city lawyer," he said, feeling embarrassed as Trina laughed.

"I'm not interested in all that. I like you for you, Elmer. You're kind and considerate, there's nothing you don't know about growing vegetables or looking after horses. My uncle says you're the best laborer he's ever had, and you can fix anything. I'm looking forward to getting to know you better," she said, still with her hand clasped in Elmer's.

He smiled broadly – he was looking forward to it, too.

"So... tomorrow at ten?" he asked, and Trina nodded.

"I'll make some apple fritters for you. They're the professor's favorite," she replied, as he walked hand in hand with her across the paddock, his heart filled with happiness at the prospect of what was to come.

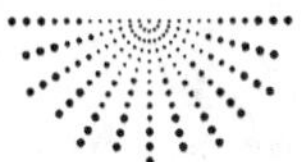

"Y ou've got enough food to feed an army," Trina's *mamm* exclaimed, as Trina heaved the picnic basket off the kitchen table.

She blushed and smiled at her *mamm*, who shook her head and laughed.

"I just want it to be nice for him, that's all. I've got a lot of making up to do, and... hey, Noah, out of there," she said, catching her brother lifting the lid of the picnic basket to take an apple fritter for himself.

"Can't I have one? You made two dozen. No one can eat two dozen apple fritters – and that's not to mention the sandwiches, the pie, the seed cake – you even made cookies," Noah exclaimed.

Trina relented.

She had gone a little overboard with her preparations, but there was no time to think about it now – Elmer had just arrived. She could see him through the window, hurrying up the path, and Starlight's head looking over the hedge from the lane. He knocked at the door and Noah went to open it.

"Good morning, Elmer. It's a lovely day for your ride together," Rebecca said, as Elmer stepped into the house and removed his hat.

Trina smiled at him. He had combed his hair and washed his face and was wearing a freshly pressed shirt.

"Are you ready? Something smells wonderful," he said, taking the picnic basket from her as they stepped out onto the porch.

"I hope you like apple fritters," Noah called out after them.

"I love apple fritters," Elmer replied, smiling at Trina as they walked along the path together.

Starlight was waiting for them patiently, and Trina patted his nose, excited at the prospect of riding him. Elmer attached the picnic basket to the saddle and helped Trina onto the horse, pulling himself up in front of her.

"Do I just hold on?" she asked.

"I won't go too fast, I promise," he said, geeing Starlight off.

They cantered along the lane, and Trina felt the wind in her hair, her arms around Elmer as they rode on, passing her aunt's smallholding before taking a path up onto the ridge.

"You can see for miles," she exclaimed.

"I love riding up here. On a clear day, you can see right across the state," he said, pointing over Faith's Creek and off into the distance.

"It's beautiful. Let's have our picnic here, shall we?" she said.

Elmer reined Starlight in and jumped down, helping Trina to the ground.

They were next to a shady oak tree, and they sat beneath its boughs as Trina unpacked the basket. There really was enough food to feed an army. Elmer marveled at the sight of everything Trina had prepared.

"Did you make all of this?" he asked.

Trina nodded, a little embarrassed. She had gone overboard.

"My *mamm* helped me. It was fun. I wanted to do something special for you – to make up for, well… you know," she said, blushing under his gaze.

"You don't have to. We just needed to start again, and it was me that jumped to conclusions," he replied, and he reached out and took her by the hand.

Trina smiled and squeezed his hand.

"Then let's agree not to do that anymore. If we ever have a problem, we'll talk about it," she said, and Elmer agreed.

They spent a pleasant few hours together on the ridge. It was a warm day, and Trina could not have felt happier than in Elmer's easy company. He talked about the horses and made suggestions for things they could do together. He was interested in her and wanted to know about her work for the professor and the things she had learned from him. In the time they spent together, Trina realized just how much she had denied herself in the happiness which should have been hers.

"We've got so much to look forward to," she said, as they packed up the picnic basket to return home.

Trina had just finished tightening the straps when a shout from along the path caused her to look up. To her surprise, Dominic was hurrying toward them, and Trina turned to Elmer in confusion.

"Is something wrong?" Elmer asked as Dominic appeared panting in front of them.

"It's my pa, he's not well. He's taken a turn for the worse. He needs you, Trina. He's had the phone taken out, I can't call for help," Dominic exclaimed.

"Oh, goodness. Quickly, let's hurry," she exclaimed, as Elmer helped her into the saddle.

"I don't know if we can carry three," he said, but Dominic shook his head.

"I can't do anything. It's you that can help – fetch the doctor, will you?" he cried.

Elmer nodded, geeing Starlight off.

They galloped along the path, and Trina clung to Elmer, anxious to reach the professor as quickly as possible.

"I'll ride on and bring Doctor Yoder back. You make sure the professor's comfortable," Elmer said, as they reached the gate into the professor's garden on Forest Hill.

Trina jumped down and watched as Elmer rode off. She hurried up the path and let herself into the house, uncertain of what she would find. She could hear the professor coughing in his study and she hurried through the door, finding him sprawled in his chair, pale and sweating.

"Oh, goodness me, Professor Lindorp. Let me help you," Trina exclaimed, as she kneeled at his side, loosening his necktie and opening his collar.

He gasped for breath, clutching at Trina's hand.

"I'm not long for this world," he said.

Trina shook her head. "Nonsense. Elmer's gone to fetch Doctor Yoder. He'll be here in no time. I'll get you some water," she said, and she rushed to the kitchen, returning a moment later with a glass which she held to the professor's lips.

Her presence seemed to comfort him, and his breathing grew a little easier. She propped him back in his chair, placing a footstool under his feet so he could lie back.

"Where's Dominic?" the professor asked.

Trina took his hand in hers and squeezed it reassuringly.

"He's on his way. He came to find us on the ridge just now. But the horse couldn't carry all three of us. Elmer brought me back here, and he's gone on to fetch Doctor Yoder," she replied, trying to calm the professor's nerves.

"Oh... all right. I don't... oh, I feel faint," he said, closing his eyes.

Trina leaped up and flung open the window. The room was stuffy, and the blast of fresh air from the garden seemed to revive the professor, who groaned and tried to turn over.

"Just stay lying back. I don't want you choking," Trina said, praying the doctor would arrive soon.

It was around twenty minutes later when she heard footsteps on the porch. The professor was half asleep, and Trina ran into the hallway and opened the door, finding Elmer and Doctor Yoder walking up to the door.

"I came as soon as Elmer told me what happened. How is he?" Doctor Yoder asked, hurrying past Trina and making straight for the study door.

"I've kept him comfortable. He's had something to drink, and the window's open, too," Trina replied, following the doctor with Elmer behind.

Doctor Yoder kneeled at the professor's side and felt his pulse. It was then that Dominic arrived, his footsteps in the hallway before his anxious face appeared at the door. He was breathless, his face red, and his shirt disheveled.

"Thank goodness you're here, Doctor," he exclaimed, as Doctor Yoder proceeded with his examination.

Trina and the others watched as Doctor Yoder administered an injection to the professor, who opened his eyes and coughed.

"Look at all these people standing around," he said.

Trina breathed a sigh of relief.

"Is he going to be all right, Doctor Yoder?" Dominic asked.

Doctor Yoder nodded. "He's had a nasty flare-up of his emphysema. It causes difficulty breathing – more so than normal. When the body can't get enough oxygen into it, the effects can be severe. It's probably been caused by a bout of flu or a chest infection. Keep him warm and rested, no exertions, and fetch me if anything gets worse," he said.

Dominic nodded.

"I was so worried. If it hadn't been for the two of you..." he said, glancing at Trina and Elmer.

"We just did what we had to do," Trina replied, smiling at Elmer, who nodded.

"That's the way we do things in Faith's Creek. We look out for one another, we're a community," he said.

Dominic smiled. "I've learned that since coming here. In the city, no one helps anyone. It's a place of strangers. But that's not the case here. Not at all. You've shown what it really means to belong to this community, and it's a community I'm glad to be a part of, too – even if I am an outsider," he replied.

Trina slipped her hand into Elmer's and smiled. She was proud of what they had done together, and it made her think again of the future they might have – a future that had begun that day. It had not occurred to her to fall in love. She had expected nothing from her aunt's introductions. But love had come on her unexpectedly, and she was rapidly falling ever more deeply into it.

"And we're glad to have you," Elmer replied, and he held out his hand to Dominic, who shook it.

Trina helped Professor Lindorp to sit up. She fetched blankets for him, lit a fire in the study hearth, and then set about making a chicken broth, leaving instructions for Dominic as to how to warm it up on the stove later that evening.

"I'll come back first thing tomorrow morning," she said, as she and Elmer stepped out onto the porch.

"You make a good team," Dominic said, smiling at them both.

Trina blushed. But it was true – she and Elmer had worked together, they had overcome their misunderstanding, and now a bright future lay ahead.

"I think we do," she replied, looking up at Elmer with a smile.

They walked together with Starlight along the lane leading back home. Trina could not have felt happier than in that moment, happy to have put their differences aside and look forward to something better for them both.

"I'm so glad we spent the day together," Elmer said, as they paused at the gate leading into Trina's garden.

"I am, too. I hope we can do it again," she replied.

Elmer nodded. "I'd like that. I'd like that a lot," he said.

Trina smiled. "Why don't you come and have dinner with us tomorrow night? You'll have to fight Noah for the apple fritters, and you might have to put up with my Aunt Leah rehearsing her distrust of the *Englischers*, but I'm sure there'd be enough to go around," she said.

Elmer nodded. "I'll be there. I'll bring something from the garden... maybe..." and now he paused, reaching over and plucking a small purple flower growing in the bed below the fence.

He handed it to her, its scent filling the air with a sweet perfume.

"To add to the rose?" she asked, and he nodded.

"And I hope there'll be a lot more flowers to come," he replied.

Now, Elmer put his arms around her, and Trina gazed up at him, their eyes meeting in a look of tender affection. He leaned forward and brought his lips to hers as they shared a gentle kiss.

She rested her head on his chest, wishing the moment could last forever, and knowing she would never forget it, but it couldn't; if they were seen there would be trouble.

"I think there's an awful lot of good things to come," Trina whispered, as she realized what was to be hers – the happiness she had always sought, the happiness she had so long denied herself, the happiness which was hers for the keeping.

EPILOGUE

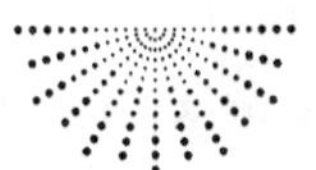

ONE MONTH LATER.

Trina finished her work. She was still enjoying it so much. Lindy had moved in as well as Dominic and the house was always filled with laughter. Though the younger couple had reinstalled the telephone and were often away Trina loved her job.

The professor was much better and having his son and daughter-in-law to be there seemed to have given him a new lease of life. Trina was also happy because she knew that Elmer would be waiting for her with Starlight. She loved spending time with him and she had a feeling that he was hiding something. Was he about to propose?

Making sure her *kapp* was tidy and her face was clean. Often, when baking, she would be covered in flour. She stepped out of the house to see Elmer's smiling face.

That smile sent a thrill through her and could chase away any raincloud. There was a grin on his face that was so delightful that she wanted to laugh, to jump into his arms and ride away on Starlight.

"You look so happy," Elmer said.

"Of course, I am, you make me happy."

His own face split into a grin that would rival the sun in its brightness. "I have a surprise for you."

Her heart stuttered for a moment, was he going to ask her here? *Nee*, that would be wrong."

"Don't look concerned," he said and took her hand. "Close your eyes."

She did and he led her from the house and around the corner. What was he doing?

She could hear Starlight stamping his feet and nickering. The horse was eager for a run. How she wanted to open her eyes but she didn't, it felt so *gut* to be held by him and to anticipate the surprise. Was it a picnic? A gift? A proposal?

"Can I open my eyes?"

"Not yet." He took her hand and held it to Starlight's neck. Stroking the horse with her hand. "Now you can open them."

Trina opened her eyes to see her hand on the coat of a palomino horse. The golden coat was dappled and silky and the silver mane was fine and beautiful. Trina turned to Elmer, a question on her lips but she couldn't form the word.

"She is yours, a gift from me. Her name is Dancer for she prances and looks like she is dancing... but you can change it if you don't like it."

Trina felt her mouth drop open. This was the most fabulous thing that anyone had ever done for her. "I don't know what to say."

He cupped her cheek with his hand and she leaned forward and kissed him briefly on the lips. That kiss filled her with possibilities but she pulled back in case they were seen.

His face was red. "There is something else I want to ask you. I was going to wait until we were up on the hill but I can't. My heart is bursting. I love you, Trina, will you marry me?"

Trina felt as if her heart had exploded out of her chest with joy. Elmer looked so shy, so unsure standing there and she wanted to pull him into her arms and tell him to never doubt her love but she couldn't move. She was frozen with joy.

Elmer dropped his head and backed away. "I'm sorry, I shouldn't have asked. You would never love a man like me."

Trina grabbed a hold of his shirt and pulled him back. She planted a kiss on his lips, no longer caring if they were seen. "I love you, Elmer, I love you more than I can say. Or course, I will marry you. I can't wait to be your *fraa*. Oh, how much I love you."

Elmer pulled her into his arms and kissed her once more before pulling back. "How about we ride over the hill and then call back to see Bishop Beiler, or do you wish to tell your *mamm* first?

"That can all wait, first I want to see if Dancer is faster than Starlight. Catch me if you can?"

With that, she climbed into the saddle and set the horse toward the hill. Soon they were racing across the fields, the wind in their faces and love in their hearts.

* * *

If you enjoyed this book you will love The Amish Landscape or read on for a preview of an amazing value box set.

LOVE, HEART AND FAMILY 30 BOOK INSPIRATIONAL BOX SET - PREVIEW

A dozen pies were cooling on the windowsill, Katy Zook had just removed three more from the oven, their sweet aroma filling the kitchen with the scent of apples and cinnamon. She looked down and smiled, for baking brought her pleasure. The pies were her pride and she was always proud of how wonderful they looked.

As they sat there all tempting, the thought of cutting into them was too much to resist. Placing two on the cooling rack, she set the other down on her workbench, taking a knife she cut it open. The aroma filled the air with apples making her stomach rumble. The filling still bubbled with heat, as she placed a slice into a dish and covered it with heavy cream.

She was just about to take a spoon from the drawer and begin to eat when a knock at the door caused her to startle. Katy was used to being alone, living in the house which had belonged to her parents for fifty years and which her grandfather had built when first they had come to join the community at Faith's Creek. When her parents died, Katy had been left alone. She made a simple living by selling the pies and pastries she was famous for, along with eggs from the chickens she kept out back.

"It's just me," came the familiar voice of her friend Susan Schrock.

Katy set down her spoon with a sigh and went to answer the door.

Susan was her usual maternal self, looking radiant and even more pregnant than the last time Katy had seen her. Susan's stomach was bulging under the plain blue dress she wore, her hair tied up and tucked beneath her *kapp*. She was carrying Rosella, her first child, in her arms and bustled inside, without waiting to be invited.

"I was just..." Katy began, and Susan raised her eyebrow.

"Eating your profits?" she asked.

Katy smiled. "Won't you sit down? I'll make some *kaffe*. Will you have a slice of pie? It's already cut," Katy said.

Susan laughed. "They smell delicious. I don't think there's a better baker than you in the whole county. Those chocolate walnut buns you made last week were delicious. Bishop Beiler couldn't stop talking about them when I saw him earlier," she said, setting Rosella down on the rug and taking a seat at the table.

"Amos Beiler is one of my best customers, he's asked for an apple turnover for next week. It's Sarah's birthday and he wants to do something special for her," Katy said, setting a kettle of water on the burner to boil.

"Samuel's like that too, he does such lovely things for me. Do you know, the other day he went out and picked me flowers from the meadow by the creek and had them in a vase waiting for me when I got home. It was the sweetest thing, I'm so lucky," Susan said, as Katy cut her a slice of pie.

The two women had been friends for many years, but their lives had taken something of a different course. While Susan was married and content with a healthy, happy child and another on the way, Katy had found little solace in the hope of marriage. Her courting year resulting in nothing but the heartache of seeing herself passed over, always ignored and rejected.

"Cream?" she asked.

Susan nodded. "It looks divine. It seems like we came at just the right moment," she said, taking the spoon which Katy offered and digging in hungrily.

"How's Rosella doing? Does she realize she's about to have a baby brother?" Katy asked.

"Or sister, I don't know what it is. I know you can find out, but I just don't think that's right. Why not let it be a surprise as *Gott* intended?" Susan said, taking another spoonful of the pie.

"A girl then a boy, isn't that what you want?" Katy asked.

Susan shrugged her shoulders. "So long as they grow up happy, healthy, and faithful I'll settle for anything," she replied, "this is good pie."

"That's the one thing I'm good at, I suppose," Katy said.

Susan frowned. "Now, I don't want to hear that. You're always putting yourself down, Katy. There are lots of things you're good at. Didn't your cross stitch win first prize at the craft fair last year? And they were falling over themselves to buy your goat's milk soaps, I've still got one and Samuel was just saying the other day how delightful it smelled and…" Susan said.

Katy interrupted her. "It's not that… I can bake and sew and craft and mend all you like, but what's the point if there's no one to share it all with," she said, glancing at Rosella, who was rolling and giggling on the rug by the stove.

"Oh, Katy, don't talk like that. You're twenty-two, hardly an old maid," Susan replied, leaning over and patting Katy on the arm.

"But I'm not exactly inundated with offers either, am I?" Katy replied, looking down at her flour-covered apron and sighing.

It was not that she was unattractive, she was pretty even, but in the years of her mother's illness and with her father gone, it was food that had become her comfort. Pies, pastries, bread, cakes, sweet treats, and savory, they had all been Katy's solace and now her figure was almost as round as Susan's. Without realizing it she had become overweight. Now, she was the subject of teasing by the local children, who would call her fat and throw sweets at her as she walked by. It upset her deeply and the more she thought about it, the worse it got.

Katy had no confidence, in herself or in the opinions of others. She was plain Katy, the baker who ate too many of her own pies, hardly an object of attraction to any man. Compared to Susan, Katy felt a failure and she knew it would have upset her mother dearly to know how unhappy her daughter was. She was an only child and if it were not for the meager living she earned selling her produce to the people of Faith's Creek she would have nothing to call her own or be proud of.

"There's someone for everyone, Katy. I believe that. Don't you?" Susan said.

Katy sighed. She knew that Susan was trying to cheer her up but at that moment, she felt nothing but despair. She had thought about it a lot recently, perhaps because she had been baking for a wedding. The happy couple seemed so very much in love that it had set her thinking about her own future too. How she longed to be that bride, to have a man to call her own, a man that would be kind and decent towards her and love her for who she was.

"I'm starting to wonder," Katy replied, finishing her slice of pie, and wondering whether it would be glutinous to cut herself a second slice.

"You'll find someone, or better still, he'll find you. Besides, you've never shown any interest in all that before, you always say you don't want children. That was delicious, by the way," Susan said, laying down her spoon.

"Another slice?" Katy asked, thinking that it would not appear as bad if Susan accepted her offer.

"I couldn't possibly, but I'll take one for Samuel. He's been out working on the farm all day, he'll be glad of it. I only wish I could bake like you. My pies always over bake on the top and stay raw on the bottom," she said, shaking her head.

"That's because you put them on a cold tray. Heat your tray first, then put the pie tin on top, that way the heat of the oven goes all around," Katy said.

Susan laughed. "See, I told you you're good at things and if the way to a man's heart is through his stomach, then you'll have the whole of Faith's Creek queueing up to marry you," Susan said, reaching down to pick up Rosella, who had started to cry.

The two women passed a pleasant morning, as Katy continued baking and Susan imparted what she referred to as 'interesting information,' which otherwise might be interpreted as gossip. When the clock struck noon, she looked up and let out a cry of exclamation, clambering to her feet and putting on her shawl.

"Is it something I said?" Katy asked.

Susan laughed. "I said I'd have Samuel's dinner on the table for half-past. I'd best get going," she said, scooping up Rosella, who had once again been playing happily on the rug.

"Take a loaf of bread and the rest of the pie. He'll not want much else if you place that in front of him. You take care now and call in anytime, I'm always happy to see you," Katy said.

"Don't be a stranger now, you're always welcome with us too. I'll see you at the service on Sunday, if not before. Don't forget, it's in Rueben Petershiem's barn this week, they're having food afterward too," she said, as Katy opened the door for her.

"I know, Almina's got me baking three cakes for her," Katy said, and with that, she waved Susan off, watching, as she made her way along the track which wound its way through the cornfields towards Faith's Creek.

She closed the door and returned to the kitchen, the lingering, sweet smell of cinnamon making her hungry once again. Susan's words were playing on her mind. She had always shied away from conversations about children, owing to her own self-belief that she would never have any. But the claim that she did not want children was false, a means of deflecting the very real desire she felt, as her maternal instincts grew. Seeing Susan so happy had made her long even more for a child and the thought that she might never have one weighed heavily on her mind.

Grab all 30 books in this great value box set for FREE with Kindle Unlimited. Love, Heart, and Family 30 Book Inspirational Collection

All my books are FREE on Kindle Unlimited

If you love Amish Romance, the sweet, clean stories of Sarah Miller receive free stories and join me for the latest news on upcoming books here

These are some of my reader favorites:

The Amish Landscape

ABOUT THE AUTHOR

Sarah Miller was born in Pennsylvania and spent her childhood close to the Amish people. Weekends were spent doing chores; quilting or eventually babysitting in the community. She grew up to love their culture and the simple lifestyle and had many Amish friends. The one thing that you can guarantee when you are near the Amish, Sarah believes is that you will feel close to God.

Many years later she married Martin who is the love of her life and moved to England. There she started to write stories about the Amish. Recently after a lot of persuasion from her best friend she has decided to publish her stories. They draw on inspiration from her relationship with the Amish and with God and she hopes you enjoy reading them as much as she did writing them. Many of the stories are based on true events but names have been changed and even though they are authentic at times artistic license has been used.

Sarah likes her stories simple and to hold a message and they help bring her closer to her faith. She currently lives in Yorkshire, England with her husband Martin and seven very spoiled chickens.

She would love to meet you on Facebook at https://www.facebook.com/SarahMillerBooks

Sarah hopes her stories will both entertain and inspire and she wishes that you go with God.

www.ingramcontent.com/pod-product-compliance
Lightning Source LLC
Chambersburg PA
CBHW071329140726
47996CB00005B/1895